D1596072

MEDUSA

S.W. GUNN

For more information contact:
2668D Columbia Ave
Tacoma, WA 98433
www.swgunn.com/greenwhale

Design by S.W. Gunn
Cover by Howard Pak and S.W. Gunn

Print ISBN 978-1-7336988-5-6
Digital ISBN None

FIRST EDITION 2020

TERMS AND PHRASES

Agora – A marketplace

Cecropia – The Acropolis

Chiton – A sleeveless tunic commonly full length for women are mid-thigh length for men.

Didrachm – A unit of coin accounting for 2 Drachma. Made of silver/weighing 8.6 grams.

Drachma –A unit of coin accounting for 6 obols. Made of silver/weighing 4.3 grams

Hellas – The name that the Ancient Greeks gave Greece (they did not call it Greece)

Himation – A mantle or wrap used as a cloak or shawl for cold weather, women would use it as a hood.

Obol – The unit of coin made of silver/weighing 0.72 grams.

Perizoma – A loincloth worn by men and women as an undergarment.

Propylaea – The gateway that leads into the Cecropia.

Schoinos – Approximately four and a half miles in distance.

Stadion – 1/8th of a Roman mile.

Strigil - A scraping device Ancient Greeks used to clean themselves with before bathing.

Strophion – An undergarment women would wear to hold their chest in place.

NOTES:

[1] - Traditionally the name 'Parthenon' was not used until much later as the Athenians just called it 'the temple' beforehand. I have choose to use the name 'Parthenon' for ease of use of the reader. I felt that it was easier for the reader to understand than 'ho naos'.

For my mother-in-law Sumintra.
Thanks for always being on my side!

PROLOGUE

Medusa was startled awake by the sound of her chicken squawking angrily about something. She sat up and looked out towards the entrance of her cave. An obviously male figure was blocking most of the outside light from entering the cave. He was wearing an unusual cap, what looked like leather armor, winged shoes, holding a sword in one hand and a very large unusual looking shield in the other. For some reason she could not see any more than the shadowy figure of the man.

Standing up she nervously asked, "Who are you?"

The man shifted his shield towards her and then looked into the shield.

He boldly stated, "I am Perseus and I am here to end you monster."

Medusa panicked. The man was not looking at her so there was no way that she could turn him to stone. She sidestepped to get away from him.

"Go away, I did nothing to you." She yelled out at him.

"You need not 'do' anything beast. I need your head as a gift."

Looking to her left and right she struggled to find something to defend herself. The nearest thing that she could find was an old battered sword sitting against the wall next to the shadowy man. He began to move closer towards her and raised his sword.

Pleadingly she attempted to explain, “I am no monster.”

The man laughed before declaring, “Of course you are. Look at you. So hideous. Your head will make a prize that will thrust me into the annals of history.”

“I am a woman cursed not a monster.”

“I do not care what you think you are. My needs are greater than your life.”

Trying to convince him she stated, “I am pregnant with my child.”

“Only more reason to end you.” He declared.

He took a few more steps closer. Medusa shifted away and towards the wall behind her. Grabbing a nearby jar filled with water she tossed it at the man. It shattered against his shield, which she realized was mirrored. She now knew how he was able to see her without turning to stone. Trying to back away from him she bumped into the back wall of the cave.

“Please just leave me alone, I just want to be left alone.” She wailed out in desperation.

“You end now.” The man angrily declared.

She spotted a flash of light flicker off to her right and then everything went black.

CHAPTER 1

"Medusa!" A voice that Medusa immediately recognized as her mother's called out loudly.

She had spent her morning working in the garden that her mother had set up before Medusa was born. They grew some of the grain, fruit, vegetables, and most of the spices that her mother would use in the bakery. Medusa spent most of her free time there tenderly keeping her small olive tree. She had been nurturing it for the last three years and it was now ready for her to finally bring to the Cecropia, the temple for the Goddess Athena. Tomorrow she would head to Athens with her older sister Euryale and her younger brother, who was named after her father Phorcys, to offer the tree to Athena. Medusa very much wanted to go alone but respectable women did not travel without a male family member. Even though she was thirteen years old her family worried about her. Medusa was blessed by the Goddess Aphrodite with very attractive and unusual features. Most Greeks had olive skin, dark hair, and brown eyes. Her skin was fair, her eyes crystal blue, and her hair was a light blonde color. It was a trait that she inherited from her father. She stood out everywhere that she went and Medusa's parents worried that some ruffian would attempt to harm her if left alone.

"Medusa!" Her mother's voice echoed out again.

She could tell that her mother was getting irritated now.

Calling out loudly Medusa declared, "I am coming mother!"

Taking one last look at her olive tree Medusa stood up and jogged back into their home. Due to her father's work, as the scribe for their town's mayor, they lived in a slightly nicer home than most of the people of Piraeus. It was a well-made building with much more space than the average home. She entered one of the back doors that led into the kitchen. Normally her mother would use the kitchen to bake for her customers, one of the larger rooms of the home was converted into a bakery for the village to sell honey cakes, and then cook supper outside. She did not ask why her mother choose to cook in the kitchen tonight and since her mother was already irritated with her, she did not ask. Medusa and her sister worked with her mother there every day. She had a half year or so before the negotiations for her arranged marriage would be completed. Because of her distinct look her father was able to find dozens of very wealthy suitors. The young man chosen, Theodosius, was the son of a very rich merchant from Athens. She was unsure what to think about being married but she knew that she would do her best to be as good a wife as she could be. As Medusa entered the kitchen she untied and then slipped her sandals off. Her mother was busy at work cooking.

"About time. I called you several times." Her mother huffily stated.

Medusa took a moment to look at her mother. She was wearing a full length wool chiton that loosely fit her and came down to her bare feet. Normally her mother would wear a dyed chiton but while working in the kitchen she wore an undyed one. Since it was her working chiton it was fastened in place with simple bronze metal fasteners on the shoulders.

"Sorry mother, I was tending to my offering for Athena."

"Right, get to work."

"Yes mother."

A rule in her mother's kitchen was to remove any jewelry Medusa or her sisters were wearing. Her mother did not want her customers to accidentally bite into a bead. Medusa removed her necklace and several bracelets, which she placed into a box set off to the side, before she got to work. She dipped her hands into the water bucket to rinse off the dirt from the garden. Like her mother, she was wearing an undyed wool chiton that fell to the floor. Unlike the heathen barbarians outside of Athens, the women of Athens were modest and did not flaunt their bodies. They let their virtuous nature as an Athenian woman speak for itself. Medusa got to work kneading the dough for the current batch of bread. Her mother was baking fish. It would be some time before her father returned home from work for supper. Many times he would have to go back to work afterwards but he always came home for meals. Her sister Euryale entered with several plates that appeared clean. No doubt their mother made her wash them for the forthcoming meal. Euryale was wearing the same chiton that everyone else had on. She had her dark brown hair tied back to keep it out of her way.

"You finally left that silly tree." Euryale declared.

Defensively Medusa responded, "It is going to be an offering. Someday it will honor Athena proudly as a tall beautiful olive tree."

"Ugh. Olive trees are ugly looking." Euryale huffily stated.

"No, they are majestic and they give us olives."

With a scoffing laugh Euryale set down the plates that she cleaned and collected a large handful of dirty ones. She was going to have to take them to the well on the other side of their home to wash them in a bucket. Medusa was very irritated with her opinion about the olive tree. They were only a week away from Euryale's wedding, Medusa could not wait to be free of Euryale's mockery and jealously. Because of Medusa's hair and eyes both of her sisters were more than a little jealous. Also growing the tree from a cutting was not easy work and Medusa put a lot of effort to baby the cutting into a tiny tree. She felt that she had every reason to be proud of it. Once it was able to, she planted it into the garden in the backyard. It was touch and go for a few weeks before her tree took root in the garden. What was even more work was convincing her parents to let her take the tree to the Cecropia to offer it to the Goddess Athena. A proper Athenian woman did not walk alone in the streets and it was even more so for Medusa. Her parents caved in and let her go if she went with both her brother and her sister. She did not care who went with her, she just wanted to offer her tree. There could be little doubt that Athena would be honored by such a fine tree. Usually people would only offer a branch, after all olive trees were valued by most Athenians since they grew olives. The fruit of these trees was a staple in the diets of most who lived in Athens. She could barely contain her excitement thinking how happy the priestesses of the temple would be to receive such a fine offering. Maybe the priestesses would plant the tree in the small courtyard within the Cecropia. She had to admit that she did not understand why there was not a symbol of the goddess there in the first place. Her only guess was that no one was willing to give the priestesses one before.

"Medusa, the dough is kneaded enough. Flatten it out and bake it." Her mother instructed.

Flushing in embarrassment, she got to working on the dough in order to flatten it. She was distracted by her own thoughts. She separated the dough into several pieces of bread. Bread was very important for every supper since her mother loved to serve soup and they used to bread to eat the soup. It was also one of Medusa's primary chores to bake it. Stethno, who was the oldest daughter, had this chore before but since she left it fell to Medusa. Father had talked about buying slaves to make up for the work load. The bakery her mother ran was much more successful than anyone thought it was going to be and the work load had gotten to be much greater than her mother, Euryale and Medusa could keep up with. Medusa imagined it would be even worse once both Euryale and Medusa were wed.

Her mother interrupted Medusa's thought with her next order, "Once you put the bread in the oven I need you to prepare the fish next."

"Yes mother."

Medusa sighed inward. She hated making the fish because it smelled funny and gutting them was always disgusting. Up to this point in her life everything that she would need to know to tend a home she had learned from her mother. She was able to grow food and prepare almost anything an Athenian would want to eat. Sewing and basic home repair such as fixing furniture were requirements for a proper Athenian wife. Putting the bread in the brick oven, she closed the wooden door. Next, she had to scale and gut the fish before rubbing a mixture of marjoram and olive oil into the flesh. Her mother always liked to bake the fish simply. Medusa then put them onto a metal plate and placed the fish into the second oven. She checked the bread, which still had some time to complete, before closing the doors.

Euryale walked by her and said, "I cannot wait to run my own home. Aiolos promised to buy a half dozen slaves so I will not have to do any these chores."

Medusa chuckled. Aiolos was the son of a banker in Piraeus. His father was a renowned for being tight in the coin purse and he did not own slaves because they were expensive to maintain. She doubted that the olive fell far from the tree. No, Medusa was confident that Euryale would be doing these chores in her own home. Her sister walked away with a grin on her face. Medusa thought that she would miss both of her sisters when she was married and moved to Athens. Her betrothed's father had already bought them a large home, along with a few slaves to maintain it. Medusa's primary purpose once married would be to provide her future husband with children and then manage the household for him. Theodosius was a few years older than she was but the one time that she met him she found him to be pleasant. He was decently fit and he clearly found her attractive, as most men who saw her did, due to her unique appearance.

Just then her younger brother came into the courtyard where the family ate and declared, "Father is coming soon. I saw him down the road."

Medusa panicked because the fish would not be done for a bit longer than it would take him to get home. It would not be ready in time and her mother would likely blame her for wasting time while tending her olive tree. Her father had always doted over her and she would hate to disappoint him. She grabbed a few more logs of wood and tossed them onto the fire that heated the oven in an attempt to speed up cooking the fish. After checking the bread, she saw that it was almost ready. After pacing for a few moments she took the bread out and hurriedly walked it back into the kitchen.

As soon as she entered her mother asked, "Your father is coming home soon, how far along is the fish?"

"I put more wood in the fire to cook it a little faster."

"Medusa! That will cause it to burn. You have to cook it very carefully when you oil it."

Her mother set down the knife that she was using to cut the vegetables and briskly walked out into the courtyard. Medusa took the bread off the baking plate and set each loaf into a basket. Her mother returned with the fish, which looked perfect.

"I saved it in time." Her mother told her.

Medusa did not say anything in response instead she came over and helped her mother transfer the fish onto a large plate. Her mother always demanded perfection of Medusa and her sisters. Stethno was ecstatic when she moved out and Euryale was ready to leave as well. Medusa was a lot more hesitant about leaving because she was the only one who would be leaving Piraeus and once in Athens she would not be able to come back to see her family. She would be alone with her new family. She met her future family when she met her betrothed and they all seemed very excited about her joining them as part of their family.

She heard her father's voice echo from the courtyard, "Wife, I have returned home."

Her mother picked up the plate with the fish and the other plate holding the vegetables before saying, "Bring the bread and soup."

She then walked out of the kitchen. Medusa grabbed the basket of bread and the large bowl of soup that her mother had made earlier. She headed out into the courtyard. Her father, brother, and Euryale where sitting in chairs by the large table in the middle of the open space. Their courtyard was surrounded by walls and all of the rooms of their home led into the courtyard. It was the center of their household.

Beaming a smile her father declared, "Ahh fish. Ceto makes the best fish in all of Piraeus."

"You flatter me husband." Her mother said softly.

The only time that her mother was kind or tender was when talking to her father and brother. Medusa loved her mother but she was a strict taskmaster on her daughters. She suspected it was because she wanted all of them to be excellent wives. Medusa set the basket with the loaves of bread on the table and then placed the large bowl next to it.

Her father instructed, "Medusa serve us our soup."

"Yes father." She responded before slowly pouring some soup into each open bowl.

First her father, then her brother, her mother, her sister and finally a bowl for herself. Setting the large bowl down, she took a seat on a wooden stool next to Euryale.

As they started to eat her mother asked, "Husband how was your day?"

"It was good. We had several traders heading to Athens arrive. They had to be tracked and the taxes applied. It was a bit of work and we are having a meeting in the andron later to discuss issues further.'

"Do you need your wine restocked?"

"No but could set some of your honey cakes for the guests."

"Of course." Her mother replied.

Medusa was slightly surprised by her father's request. Usually he would not ask for anything but his wine in the andron unless he had important guests. She was quite curious who was coming. The male guests who would visit her father were not allowed access to the rest of the home where the women stayed so she would never know. A very wicked thought crossed Medusa's mind. Usually the men visiting her father would arrive as the sun had started to set. She decided that she would attempt to sneak a peek at them and see for herself just who these important guests were. Dipping a piece of her bread into the bowl of soup she took a bite. It was very good. Hopefully she would be able to provide her own family with equally as good food as her mother always did.

They ate in silence for a moment before her father declared, "I spoke with my brother, Andronicus and he has offered to send his oldest son Demosthenes with Medusa and Euryale tomorrow for their trip to Athens."

Medusa was surprised when her brother angrily said, "Father, I can take care of them myself!"

None in the family ever talked back to her father so she gasped loudly when her brother spoke. Her mother and sister seemed just as shocked.

Keeping his cool her father replied, "Of course you could son but I need you to come with me to work. The mayor has asked that I start your training so you may replace me someday as the town's scribe."

Her brother looked very shameful as he glanced downward at his bowl before he said softly, "I am sorry father."

"There is no need to apologize. It is a man's duty to protect their women and you were just expressing your desire to live up to your role as a man of this family but part of that protection is to ensure that we remain employed."

Her mother announced, "Tomorrow I will not be opening the bakery since both of my daughters will be in Athens."

"Ceto I have already began to search for slaves to assist you in the house and bakery. It will cost us several drachma for three young women."

"Thank you husband."

Her father grinned at her as he nodded. The rest of the meal was ate in silence. Once everyone finished eating supper Medusa helped collect up the bowls and leftovers. All of the scraps would be tossed out in a small compost pile near the garden. After cleaning up Medusa was released for the evening by her mother. Now it was just a matter of waiting.

CHAPTER 2

After Medusa finished cleaning up from supper the sun was already beginning to set. She made sure to tend to her olive tree by giving it a little water. Having to be careful not to overdo the water it got, she measured every drop constantly. She anticipated resolving her curiosity about her father's upcoming meeting quite a bit. Usually during this time of night her mother, brother, and sister would each take a turn bathing and then go to bed. Medusa generally bathed and would go to bed as well but she was just too curious to pass up this opportunity. As it started to get dark so she passed through the courtyard and into the bathing room, women were not allowed to be outside at night for their own safety. Moving quickly she filled the stone tub with hot water and then stripped off her clothing. The knowledge about proper bathing was a gift from the gods. Before bathing she rubbed pumice and olive oil over her body. Then she used a bronze strigil to remove the mixture. It was all part of keeping the body pure. Once she was done she stepped into the tub. Hot water cleansed the body. It kept a person healthy and strong. It also felt really good. Medusa dipped her head into the water to rinse her hair. Her mother constantly reminded her not to be prideful over her unique appearance and Medusa tried to but she had to admit that it was very hard to do on sometimes. Once clean, she used a strip of cloth to dry herself off. Then she wrapped a strophion around her chest and tied her perizoma around her waist before slipping on a clean chiton. After fastening it, she headed off to the bedroom that she shared with Euryale.

As she laid down Euryale declared, "When I am the mistress of my home I will not be going to bed so early."

Medusa said nothing in response.

"Why can women not have meetings with other women?"

A question that Medusa had no answer for. The men had work that required meetings. Women's work was always in the home. She had heard stories of the wealthiest women of Athens holding big events that they would attend but that was not something done in Piraeus. Maybe once she was married and living in Athens she could find out but for now she just wanted silly Euryale to go to sleep so she could sneak out.

"Why am not surprised that you do not know?" Euryale commented sarcastically.

Not wanting to get into a fight with Euryale again Medusa said nothing. Her sisters always treated her as though she was stupid but she thought it was jealousy. Her father had generally pampered her not only because she she had her father's hair and eyes but also because was the youngest daughter.

"I am going to sleep." Euryale finally declared.

Medusa guessed that she gave up since Medusa was not going to argue with her. After a bit of a wait, the sound of Euryale's deep and even breathing echoed through the room. Medusa had to stop herself from snorting out a laugh. Euryale snored in her sleep and if she was ever told about it Medusa suspected that she would be mortified. Even with all of the minor abuse Euryale gave her, she could not bring herself to tell Euryale about the snoring. It was now time for Medusa to make her move. She was confident that her mother was fast asleep so she decided to peek and make sure that her brother was as well. He had notoriously snuck out more than a few times at night to play in the courtyard. Slipping out of her bed, she cautiously walked towards the entryway into the courtyard. Peeking out the doorway she saw that the courtyard was empty and no torches were lit. A clear sign that no one was awake. Sliding along the wall she stepped carefully to the entryway of her brother's room. Unlike the sisters, he got a room all to himself. It was his luck of not having a brother. She stopped near the entryway and listened. After a few moments she could hear her brother breathing evenly. He was sound asleep.

"Let us go hear what father is talking about." She whispered evilly to no one in particular.

Moving even more cautiously and slowly than before she crept up to the door of the andron. It was the only interior room that had a door. The only doors otherwise were on the exterior of their home. As she got closer she could hear muffled voices. The walls of her home were too thick to hear what they were saying so she was going to have to go right up to the door. As she got up to the door she could finally hear what was being said.

"Phorcys we must find unique ways to ensure that all of the taxes are being collected on visitors heading to Athens. It is our only way to ensure we can meet the taxes being placed upon us by King Menestheus. His involvement with both the Spartans and the Trojans has cost all of us dearly."

"I understand Paramonos but we cannot just raise taxes on the ships docking in Piraeus or they will go elsewhere."

Her father sounded very concerned. Clearly there was much more going in Piraeus and Athens than she was aware of.

A third voice, which she did not recognize, said, "Maybe we need to get more creative."

The first voice who she knew was someone named Paramonos asked, "What did you have in mind Seleukos?"

"Perhaps we could charge a toll to people leaving Piraeus? Something small that few would miss heading to Athens, perhaps just one obol?"

She was so fascinated by the conversation that Medusa took a seat on the ground next to the door.

The voice that her father called Paramonos answered, "Simply brilliant! Most of our citizens rarely leave the village so we would not receive much complaint about such a small toll. I will bring it to the council tomorrow for consideration."

Medusa sighed heavily since the last thing that she needed was some silly toll keeping her from bringing her olive tree to the Cecropia tomorrow.

The man named Seleukos said, "Phorcys this honey cake is delicious, do you have any more?"

"Of course." Her father answered.

Medusa panicked as she started to stand. She was unable to escape before her father opened the door of the andron and stumbled right over her!

"What the!" Her father said as he caught himself before falling.

Although she had moved he clipped her left knee. As he righted himself she stood up. She was caught and only hoped that her mother was not wakened by the noise.

"Medusa, what are you doing?" Her father asked sternly.

She flushed a bright red before telling him, "I am sorry father I was just curious."

He shook his head at her before stating firmly, "Daughter this discussion is not for women's ears."

Before she could reply her mother came out, with her hair a tangled mess, and asked, "What is going on here?"

She was doomed. Medusa was about to get into a whole lot of trouble and likely her trip to the Cecropia was in danger of being canceled.

His father was the first to answer, "Sorry to awake you wife. I accidentally bumped into Medusa here. I was going to get some more of your wonderful honey cakes for my guests and I think that she was headed to the bathroom. I did not see her in the dark courtyard and knocked her down."

Sighing heavily mentally Medusa quickly nodded at her father's lie. She was always his favorite, no doubt because of her appearance coming from him.

Her mother looked thoughtful for a moment before saying, "Very well. Husband let me get you those honey cakes."

Once her mother was out of sight her father tenderly brought his right hand up to her left cheek before saying, "My sweetest daughter you must learn that each of us has our place in the eyes of the gods. A woman's place is one of the most important in the world. Anyone can be a laborer but only women, who hold the highest place in the eyes of the gods, can bear and tend to children. Our society would die without children to further it. Do you understand?"

"Yes father."

He grinned widely at her before saying, "You have always been special. I love you daughter."

"I love you too."

"Give me a hug and go to bed. You have a busy day tomorrow."

She gave him a tight hug, which he returned. Once she let go he grinned at her. She smiled bashfully before walking back to her room. Her father was always so amazing. Of all of her family she was going to miss him the most once she was married. Visions of the exciting trip to Athens tomorrow swam through her mind before she drifted off to sleep.

* * * * *

Medusa woke the next morning when her sister nudged her to wake up. The women always woke up first so they could prepare breakfast. She flipped her feet off her low set bed before standing up. After going to the bathroom she washed her hands as she entered the kitchen. Her mother was working on making some bread and Euryale was preparing the dishes.

"Medusa take over here while I prepare the wine for breakfast."

"Yes mother."

As her mother moved away from the small table Medusa began to knead the dough. Her mother poured some wine into two cups. One for her mother and one for her father. Unlike the barbarians of other cities, Athenians added water in their wine. Her mother poured some water into several other cups for Medusa and her siblings. After Medusa finished kneading the dough she formed it into loaves and then placed the dough onto a metal plate. Euryale had started the fire for the oven out in the courtyard so Medusa was able to place the plate into the oven. This time she watched the bread closely. After yesterday's mistake she was not going to get onto her mother's bad side by making another error. Taking the bread out of the oven she transferred the loaves into the basket. Breakfast was one of the easier meals to prepare since Athenians were not big eaters, although she heard her sisters gossiping that the wealthiest were an exception with some of them even being fat. She brought the basket of bread to the table in the middle of the courtyard. Her brother was already awake and playing with one of his toys, a wooden kopis sword. Every morning normally her brother would go to school after breakfast but now he was going to learn to be a scribe just like their father. Both her mother and sister were sitting down at the table, no doubt waiting patiently for her father to finish bathing. Unlike the rest of the family he bathed in the morning since he would be gone most of the day.

As Medusa sat down in her seat her mother said, "After breakfast we will wait for Demosthenes to arrive before you both head off to Athens. You are both to listen to every instruction he gives and I want both of you to wear a himation over your heads the entire time that you are there."

"Yes mother." Both Euryale and Medusa responded in unison.

After a bit of a pause Medusa asked, "Mother after breakfast may I transfer my tree to a clay pot?"

"Of course, both of you are to wash up and I want each of you to wear an undyed chiton."

"But mother!" Euryale exclaimed.

No doubt Euryale wanted to wear her finest garb to show off their father's wealth. The opportunities to wear their embroidered chitons were rare. Medusa owned one with elegant embroidery along the lower hem of it but she had never worn it for anything other than to try it on. She was planning to wear it for her wedding.

"No Euryale. I do not want attention to be drawn to you."

"Is it because of Medusa?" She asked huffily.

Medusa frowned. She was tired of Euryale blaming her for everything bad.

"No. It is because your father gave me these instructions and we will follow his instructions fully."

Euryale did not look very happy at all but she said nothing in response to her mother's declaration. Medusa noticed that her sister had gotten more and more argumentative as her wedding day grew closer. It was something that she promised herself she would not do once the date for her wedding was set. Her father exited the bathroom and confidently walked up to the table. Following her mother, Medusa stood up. Her father sat down, which Medusa, her mother, and sister all took a seat in response. Her brother dropped his sword that he was playing with before running up to the table and sitting down.

Her mother told him, "Phorcys go wash your hands."

Standing up her brother responded, "Yes mother."

He ran off into the kitchen and after a few moments returned. As her brother walked back into the courtyard he was wiping his hands dry on his tunic. Once he sat down her father reached over and grabbed a loaf of bread. He broke a piece of the bread off and dipped it into his wine before taking a bite. Taking the lead of her father, the rest of the family began to eat. Her father talked about how excited he was to teach her brother how to be a scribe for the village but Medusa was daydreaming about the trip to Athens to pay much attention to what he was saying. She had not been this excited about anything since she met her betrothed. Once they finished breakfast Medusa and her sister cleaned up the small mess. As her father left for work, with her brother, he gave each of them a hug and then a soft kiss on her mother's cheek. After her father left Medusa tied on her sandals and took a clay pot out into the garden. She had a metal slat to dig up the tree, which she did as carefully as she could. Once the tree was in the pot, with enough dirt to keep it in place, she carried it back into the kitchen. Setting down the pot on the dirt floor of the kitchen, she untied her sandals and picked her pot again. As she brought the pot into the courtyard her mother gave her a smile. Medusa grinned widely at her.

"I do not tell you this much Medusa but I am proud of you honoring the gods in this way before your wedding. I am certain that they will bless your marriage."

"Thank you mother."

"Set your pot down and go clean up."

"Yes mother."

Setting down her pot, Medusa went back into the bedroom she shared with Euryale. She saw that Euryale was already almost dressed. Moving quickly she unlatched the fasteners on her chiton before slipping it off. Changing all of her clothing she got dressed again before wrapping a himation over her head to cover her face. The idea of the himation was to cover her hair, which she had tied into a tight bun on the back of her head, and her face. Medusa knew her father ordered the himation for her protection but she was glad that her mother put her foot down on Euryale's complaints.

"Alright, let us go." Euryale said.

Medusa followed behind her as they headed out into the courtyard. To her surprise Demosthenes was already waiting. He was about nineteen years old. Like most men his age he had a patchy and not quite complete beard. His black hair was short and he was wearing a shorter version of the same chiton her family wore. It was dyed a dull red color, most likely from some berries. She was slightly surprised to see that he had a sword tucked into the belt wrapped around his waist that was holding his chiton tightly against his body.

After giving both Euryale and Medusa a hug her mother instructed, "Both of you listen to Demosthenes and keep to yourselves. Keep your himation over your head and your eyes down."

"Yes mother." Both responded in unison.

"Follow me." Demosthenes instructed.

Medusa followed closely behind Euryale through the main doors of their home.

CHAPTER 3

It had been several months since the last time Medusa was allowed to leave the family home. That time they went to Athens as well but it was to visit her future husband's family as the final part of the arrangement for their marriage. Theodosius' parents were quite excited when they finally met Medusa. She guessed that she must have been everything that they were told she was. It was likely her hair and eyes that sealed the marriage. She was completely impressed by the extravagance of both Athens and her future family's home. No one in Piraeus came close to their wealth. From what Medusa gathered once they saw her the negotiation was changed completely. Normally the family of brides would pay a dowry price. Once word got out within the families of the wealthy Athenians it became a negotiation for who would pay her father a dowry for the right to marry her. Medusa only found out all this by snooping on a conversation between her sisters, both of which were very unhappy about it for some reason. She sneakily glanced from her left to right as best as she could while holding her head down.

Euryale whispered, "It is exciting to be free of our prison."

Medusa giggled in response. She had to admit that it was exhilarating. So rarely were women of any status allowed freedom outside of their home, and never without male family members. She spotted a few other women but could tell by their dress and their tanned skin that they were of a lower class.

As they started to head out of Piraeus their cousin Demosthenes asked, "How long will you be in the temple?"

Keeping her head down Medusa answered, "It should not take long cousin. I just need to pray to Athena and offer her this olive tree."

"As though anyone does that. Why did you not bring an olive branch like everyone else?" Euryale asked.

Medusa could hear the disdain in Euryale's voice. Medusa doubted that she wanted to even come with her to Athens but it did not matter to Medusa because she was going through with her plans. Athena was the patron of the city of Athens and Medusa had no doubt that by honoring her in with a beautiful tree Athena would bless Medusa's upcoming marriage with fruitful success and many children.

Demosthenes then said, "It greatly reflects on her to honor Athena in such a way. It is rare that anyone offers anything more than a branch of an olive tree. I wish I had thought of it."

Trying not to be too arrogant Medusa beamed a smile at Euryale, who responded by responding silently with a dirty look. It reminded Medusa that she was ready for Euryale to hurry up and get married. She turned away and looked out at the crowd. Her father's home was close to the outskirts of Piraeus heading towards Athens so she had to turn around to see people. Off in the distance she spotted over a dozen people, all wearing chiton of varying conditions. She spotted a few wealthy men wearing dyed chiton and others who were not so wealthy wearing undyed ones. Her mother made both her and Euryale wear undyed clothing, which Medusa almost wished that she did not but her mother knew best. The walk out of Piraeus was pretty quick and before long they were on the pathway heading towards Athens. The path was marked by smooth plain stones that have been set into the ground to allow carts to be pulled by mules. Piraeus was the most significant port for Athens. She had not seen it but she heard her father mention a few times that there was a large garrison of soldiers in town to protect the town from possible attacks. Most of what Medusa learned about the outside world came from her snooping on her father and her sister's gossip. She was utterly fascinated by what was going on outside her home. It was probably something that would only get worse once she was married and living in Athens.

Euryale commented, "It is lovely out today."

Medusa glanced up and looked into the sky. There were no clouds and like Euryale said, it was very nice outside. The sun was out and it was warming quickly. The harvest season had just started and the weather was sunny with the occasional rain to help grow crops. Taking a deep breath she enjoyed the walk. Athens was about a schoinos away from Piraeus so it was a good thing that they had such nice weather to make the trip in.

Her cousin responded, "Yes it is. When your father came to mine asking for a male to take the both of you to Athens my father was upset but I leapt at the chance to go to Athens."

"Why?" Medusa asked out of curiosity.

Laughing heartily Demosthenes answered, "While you are in the Parthenon[1] I am going down to the agora. There is much to see while there."

Euryale quickly asked, "Can I go with you? I have no desire to sit around in the Parthenon while she kisses up to Athena."

Medusa gave her a mean look. Demosthenes laughed heartily.

Once he finished laughing he told Euryale, "Yes, you can but you need to stay close to me."

"I will."

"Medusa, you will stay in the Parthenon until we return. Of course I'll have you both back home in time to prepare supper for your father."

Medusa nodded at him. She promised her mother to listen to her cousin, especially since he was helping her go offer her tree to Athena. Thankfully the tree was small so it would not be a heavy burden for the trip. As they continued walking Euryale began grilling Demosthenes with questions about Athens. She was just as curious about it but she did not have Euryale's boldness to ask so she walked along quietly listening as Demosthenes answered each question that he could. She found his story about the time that he spent in Athens learning how to be a soldier fascinating.

After he was done training he was sent back to Piraeus to live there. She had only seen him a few times at her home when he was visiting her father so all of this was new information to her. They continued to walk along with only the occasional person or group heading away from Athens and towards Piraeus. One group of note was a caravan of mules and carts hauling what she guessed was something to be shipped out of the port. Of course she was purely guessing since she so rarely left her father's home. The rest of the walk was a bit boring, even with the lovely weather. After a while she could see the city of Athens in the distance. The outskirts of the city were made up of poorly constructed small buildings that she guessed were homes for many poor people and slaves. Dozens of tufts of smoke wafted over the buildings. Many of the outer buildings were made from sun-dried bricks, a sign of low income due to their inferior quality. As they got closer to Athens she spotted dozens of buildings closer to the center of the city that were made of marble. A person of wealth would always use marble for their buildings since it was plentiful in Hellas and was of high quality. Her father's home was made of marble and the home that her future husband's family bought them was made from marble as well. As they approached the outskirts she spotted large crowds of people moving about.

"Look at them all!" Euryale exclaimed.

Demosthenes chuckled at her before saying, "Athens is the most important of cities and it always draws a crowd."

Medusa was impressed by the number of people but she had seen these crowds the last time that she was in Athens. It was so populated that no one seemed to notice or care as Demosthenes led Medusa and her sister through the carved pathways. There was two deep ruts on the sides of the pathways, which she guessed they were from mule pulled carts.

Once they fully entered the city Euryale complained, "It smells here."

"In the poorer areas they tend to dump their chamber pots directly into the gutters by the street. I believe every once in a while water is ran through the gutters to try and clean it out."

It was foul smelling, thankfully in Piraeus the mayor required people to pour water after every time they dumped their chamber pots. Also, the lower number of people probably made a big difference. As they continued along the crowded streets Medusa noted that it was becoming quite hilly. She made the walk easily to Athens but the hills in the city was making it a bit of a challenge. Off to her left she spotted several impressive pure white marble buildings. The first thing that really caught her eye was a massive theatre. Even the seating appeared to be made of marble.

Demosthenes must have seen her facial expression because he stated, "That is the theatre of Dionysus."

He then pointed up the hill beyond the theatre before stating, "And that is the Parthenon."

Looking up to where he was pointing Medusa gasped lightly. During her last visit they had taken a different route and she had not seen it before. The Parthenon was a tall building with long beautiful white marble columns that shone brightly as light reflected against them. She guessed that the Priestesses of the temple probably worked hard to maintain the beauty of it. The roof of the building had carvings that seemed to depict servants of Athena worshiping her. As they made their way around the hill that the Parthenon stood on she was equally impressed with the homes of the wealthy that was built alongside it. No doubt the richest of the rich lived here. Finally they circled around towards the front of the Propylaea, the gateway into the Parthenon itself. There was a large crowd of men conversing with each other. The only person she casually noted while looking with her head somewhat down was a large older man hovering off in the distance. He was looking directly at them, which she found a little unnerving. Medusa shifted closer to her cousin and then followed him as he went up the long flight of stairs that led to the Propylaea. Medusa could feel the excitement starting to build within her. She had worked so hard for this little olive tree and finally her plan was about to come to fruition. It was almost unbearable. As they passed through the Propylaea a sense of calm struck her. She saw dozens of priestesses walking around, some of which were performing what she guessed were their daily chores. A slightly older woman wearing a very plain looking chiton approached them. Her hair was dark brown, as where her eyes, and her skin was lightly tanned.

"Welcome to the temple of Athena. Do you need assistance?"

As the male family member Demosthenes was the one to answer her inquiry, "Yes. My cousin Medusa wishes to offer her olive tree to Athena as a token of honor before her wedding."

The priestess grinned widely before declaring, "A whole olive tree? I have little doubt that Athena will be greatly pleased by your tribute."

Turning to look at Euryale, who seemed quite dour, Medusa smiled widely.

"Come with me my friends." The priestess said.

Demosthenes answered, "My other cousin and I must go to the agora. Will Medusa be safe with you here?"

"Of course. The Parthenon is a haven for all women and none would dare violate that."

"Thank you priestess." Demosthenes said before giving Medusa a wave as he continued speaking, "Medusa stay here until we return."

"Yes cousin." She told him.

As he walked with away with Euryale in tow the priestess said to Medusa, "Come with me. I will take you to the statue of Athena so you may bring her your offering. I do have a question for you."

"Yes?"

"We have always wanted to plant an olive tree to honor Athena but we have not yet been successful as every branch brought to us as an offering tended to be too old or damaged. Could we plant your tree within the grounds of the Parthenon?"

Medusa beamed with excitement. There would have been nothing that could have made her happier than knowing her tree would take root and grow on these holy grounds.

Almost a little too excitedly she answered, "Of course!"

The priestess chuckled before instructing, "Follow me."

Medusa followed closely behind the priestess as she began walking towards the Parthenon. It was much more beautiful up close than it appeared to be in the distance. She spotted a few other priestesses walking around the courtyard. Medusa glanced upwards to look at the main entryway of the temple. A sense of nervousness began to overwhelm her. It was quite exciting to be here. She sidestepped a large standing marble basin filled with water that was positioned near the entrance of the Parthenon.

The priestess stopped at the entrance and instructed, "Remove your sandals here."

Giving her a nod, Medusa set her pot down and untied both of her sandals. The priestess removed her sandals. Picking up her pot Medusa followed the Priestess onto the pure white marbled floor of the Parthenon. It was cool to the touch when her feet made contact with it. As she stepped down the steps to the proper floor of the temple she was stunned by the massive statue of a woman standing on a white marble pedestal with what looked like a gold embossed procession of various people carved into it. The pedestal itself came to midway up to Medusa's chest and the detail on the figures was amazing to her. The statue of the woman on the pedestal was carved out of white marble and was wearing a pure gold chiton. On her breast was pendant with a scowling face that had its tongue sticking out. It was hideous looking. Resting on the ground and being held by the statue was a massive golden shield. Next to the shield was a huge golden snake and resting on the ground was the handle end of a spear with the tip of the spear resting against the woman's shoulder. The woman was holding out her right hand with her palm up and standing in her palm was a tiny winged man holding a branch of olive leaves. Upon the head of the woman was a pure gold helmet with five points, which Medusa could not tell what they meant. The woman's hair was made of gold.

"Young lady please remove your himation within the temple."

Nodding at her Medusa unwrapped her himation. The priestess gasped at her hair.

"You have golden hair!" She exclaimed.

"Yes. I got it from my father."

"I have never seen hair like that before. May I touch it?"

Medusa was more than slightly puzzled. No one had ever asked to touch her hair before. Deciding it could not hurt anything she nodded at her. The priestess reached out and cautiously touched her tight bun.

"It feels the same as any other's hair."

"Other than the color it is the same." Medusa stated factually.

Giving a nod the priestess then said, "I will leave you alone with Athena. Place your beautiful tree on the pedestal at her feet and leave it there as an offering. At the end of the day we priestesses will tend to it before it is planted on the western porch of the Erechtheion."

The priestess smiled at Medusa before turning away and walking out of the temple.

CHAPTER 4

Grinning widely Medusa brought her small potted olive tree up to the massive statue and placed it directly in front of the statue on the pedestal. The fact that the priestesses were going to plant her tree nearby made her very happy. She was not entirely sure what she should be doing because her parents had focused all their time with her on what she needed to know to be a great wife for her future husband. Medusa decided that maybe it would be best to sit down and just quietly contemplate about what was to come for her. Being married itself was fine but she was more excited about the prospect of living in Athens. It was such a significantly different place than Piraeus. She also was very curious about being a mother. Her mother had told her so much and while her mother was stern when it came to chores, she was very open when it came to answering questions. Especially everything about bearing children and raising them.

Suddenly a voice behind her said, "Well, what do we have here?"

The voice was of a man and his voice was course with very unusual tone to it. She was not even sure if he was from Athens. Turning her head she saw who was speaking and immediately recognized him. It was the man who was looking at her before she went up the steps of the Propylaea. She started to begin to panic because there was no one in sight to help her. Quickly moving she stood up. The man smiled. His teeth looked horrible to her, along with the rest of him. The best she could guess was that he was more than a little bit older than her father with his scraggly looking white hair and messy looking beard. His chiton was undyed and heavily stained. It was obvious that he rarely bathed. She noticed that he was not wearing sandals at all.

"You are quite the lovely little thing." He commented.

His facial expression was one of lust. She frowned before trying to take a step away from him. The speed in which he moved to cut off her escape around the statue of Athena was quite quick. She stumbled backwards to get away from him. He smelled heavily of sea water.

Yelling as loud as she could Medusa screamed, "Help! Is someone out there?"

The man chuckled at her before saying, "No one is here."

She began to panic as she tried to pull away from him and run for the entrance of the Parthenon. Right as she was about to make it to the steps she felt his hand grab her arm just above her elbow, which she screamed once again in panic. Flailing wildly to get away she lashed out as much as she could to fend off the man but her efforts seemed to be useless. The man grabbed her arm roughly and pulled her closer towards him. The salty smell was overwhelming. She continued to scream out loudly, desperately hoping that someone would hear her and save her from the brute. Thinking back to the many tales her mother had told her about strange men she started to kick wildly to try and escape.

"You are a feisty one. It is just going to make this more fun." The man snarled.

The flailing kicks that she lashed out at the man struck him several times and yet he seemed unaffected. He was able to grab her other arm with his free hand before pulling her directly up against him. Now closer to him she could smell him even more so and the salt water smell was mixed with his unpleasant body odor. She continued to struggle while trying to escape but was starting to get tired. All of her efforts seemed to be useless.

Inhaling deeply he told her, "You smell so good."

"Let me go." She told him with her voice shaking in fear.

She started to cry having given up fighting since it just seemed to making her tired.

"Oh I will, once I have taken you. It is rare to find one with golden hair."

Between her sobs she cried out, "Please leave me alone."

As the man started to push her to the marble floor of the temple Medusa renewed her efforts to escape. She started screaming and flailing as much as she could with all the effort that she could muster.

"Yes, keep fighting." The man told her with a chuckle.

Attempting to rock her body did nothing as she hit the floor. He had to let her go initially to lower her so she tried to wriggle free and escape. His iron grip got a hold of her left ankle before he dragged her back underneath him. Using her hands she swung wildly at his head. Her right hand hit the side of his head, which hurt her hand but seemed to have no effect on him. Pressing himself down onto her, she was now pinned under his heavy body. She tried to move in any way and could not. His weight was even making it hard for her to breath. Now she was sobbing uncontrollably. The man grabbed both of her wrists and pinned them together with one hand just above her head.

Between sobs she wailed out, "Please leave me alone."

Giving her a little chuckle he stated, "Oh I plan to, once I have finished."

She felt one of his hands pulling up the bottom of her chiton. With renewed effort she tried to push him away but she was unable to move him. Fatigue was starting to weaken her arms and legs.

"This is going to feel so good." The man lustily stated.

At this point he had her chiton nearly up to her waist and she could feel his very rough hand slowly moving up the inside of her leg. Right as he tried to pull on her perizoma she fought again with renewed effort.

"Yes, I was worried you had surrendered." He said.

Using his free hand he roughly slapped down her one free leg and then began running his hand along her thigh.

Desperate for any help she again bellowed out between deep gulping sobs, "Someone please save me from this brute!"

He chuckled at her before firmly stating, "No one is going to save you."

Suddenly a blinding light struck the entire room. It was so bright that Medusa's eyes were swimming and she could see nothing. She felt the man shift and release her wrists so she wriggled and squirmed away from the man. Once she was no longer underneath him she slid along the marble floor by pushing away with her feet until her back struck into something hard. She guessed that it was the wall of the temple. Blinking several times she tried to clear her vision.

A strong female voice echoed within the temple, "Who dares desecrate my temple?"

Medusa's eyes finally cleared and now she could see the woman for herself. The woman stood much taller than any man and was wearing a full length golden colored chiton. It had gold embossed fasteners holding it in place. She could not see the woman's face due to the fact she was wearing a masked helmet. In one hand she had a long spear and in another a shield. There seemed to be a glowing beam of light that shone all around her.

The woman spoke again, "Answer the Goddess Athena now mortals."

Oddly enough, the man simply laughed at her. Medusa was stunned into silence from what she was seeing.

"I said, who dares desecrate my temple with this vile act between a couple?"

Medusa panicked when she realized that standing before her was Athena. Medusa initially thought Athena was there to save her but it dawned on her that Athena thought that she was with the foul man.

Fearfully Medusa started to speak, "I am not with…"

The woman's booming voice cut Medusa off, "I care not for your excuses. I curse the both of you for daring to spoil this holiest of all of holy temples."

Right as the woman gestured with her hand holding the spear Medusa felt something strike her chest. It knocked the wind out of her and caused her to tilt over to her side. The man simply laughed loudly.

"Niece you cannot curse me."

The woman's facial expression was not visible but her voice made it clear she was angry as she said, "Poseidon you cannot enter my temple and defile it. I will personally run my spear through you."

Giving a hearty laugh the man said, "Unlikely."

He then simply vanished out of sight.

The woman who called herself Athena growled out, "I shall."

She disappeared as well leaving Medusa alone. Her breath was starting to come back. Maybe she would be fine since the man was gone. A sharp and very sudden pain struck Medusa's head. It felt like someone hit her in the head with a stone except instead of one spot it was all of her head, excluding her face. The pain was so overwhelming that she screamed out and began writhing to try and wriggle free of the suffering. Whatever Athena did to hurt immensely. She rolled to try and help free herself of the pain but nothing seemed to work. Reaching up to grasp her head she felt her hair fall off into her hand. Even with the pain of whatever happened she could see clumps of hair through her tear blurred vision. Unusual bumps began to form on her head. Finally the pain had gotten so bad that Medusa's vision went black.

* * * * *

Painfully Medusa opened her eyes. She was looking upwards at the ceiling of the Parthenon. The marble beneath her was cold. An echoing sound of what sounded like a snake rattled in her ear. She moved quickly in fear as she raced to stand up. Glancing around, she could not see any snakes. What she did see that concerned her was several large clumps of her yellow hair sitting on the ground. Right as she reached up to feel her head she heard a loud scream coming from the entrance of the Parthenon. As Medusa turned to look at who was screaming she saw the priestess who had brought her up to the pedestal. She was looking at Medusa while she was screaming and oddly enough, as Medusa looked at her her voice seemed to gargle her scream silent. After a brief moment the woman's skin started to turn a very unusual light gray color before her eyes went gray, freezing her face with a look of abject horror. She stayed frozen in that exact position with her facial expression unchanged. Medusa was very confused as to what had just happened. She still heard snakes nearby hissing but was unable to spot any around her. Ignoring that she cautiously walked towards the priestess. The chiton the priestess was wearing was normal but as Medusa reached out and touched her arm she realized that her skin was now stone! Something changed this priestess into a statue. Medusa glanced from side to side to see if anyone else was there. No one was there. More snakes began hissing from above her. She jumped from the sound and glanced up to try and avoid them. There was nothing above her. It was very confusing. Suddenly a snake came into her vision from her right, she jumped, almost diving, to her left to get away from it. Glancing back to where the snake was she saw nothing. It was all quite confusing. She decided that it was time to leave the Parthenon to get away from the snakes and if that man came back. Walking over to her sandals, which she slipped on, she picked up her himation and hurried out as quickly as she could. As she stepped out of the temple she spotted several priestesses walking around. Her first question was wonder where they were when Medusa was screaming for help a few moments ago. Suddenly one of the priestesses screamed out in fear. Medusa looked at her and once their eyes locked the woman's scream gagged into silence before her skin turned the same gray color as the priestess in the Parthenon. After another half moment her eyes turned to the stone color as well. She was now a statue wearing clothing instead of a priestess. Medusa was extremely confused. Glancing around, she saw several other people looking at her in utter fear.

One nearby woman yelled out, "It is a monster, run!"

Others began to scream and run as fast as they could out of the Cecropia and through the Propylaea. Another of the priestesses looked into Medusa's eyes and she seemed to turn to stone the second they locked eyes. Medusa was very confused about what was happening.

This time a nearby man was pointing behind Medusa as he yelled, "It is hideous. Get away now!"

Right as she looked at the man he yelled out. "It is coming for me!"

He turn to run towards the Propylaea but like the others seemed to turn to stone while looking towards her. Panicking Medusa turned to look behind her to see the monster that he was pointing at. There was nothing there. Something very odd was going on and she was more confused than ever. She still heard snakes all around her but could not see a single snake. The courtyard around the Parthenon was now clear of everyone but Medusa. Standing next to the marble basin that was near the entrance she casually glanced down at it and was repulsed by what she saw. It appeared to be her but her hair was now gone and in its place was now a large mass of snakes. The reflection was clearly her as she saw her blue eyes but it made no sense to her. She rubbed her eyes in disbelief, surely the reflection was just something amiss. Opening her eyes again she looked back into the basin. Nothing had changed. The reflection in the basin was her but with snakes for hair in place of her yellow hair. She remembered the clumps of hair she saw back in the Parthenon. Turning back towards the Parthenon she ran back in. Her hair was just as she remembered it, sitting on the floor where she was at when Athena yelled at her. There was enough yellow hair to have covered all of Medusa's head. It was then that Medusa realized what had happened. Athena had cursed her. Her whole life was in shambles so she fell to her knees and picked up two clumps of hair with her hands. She started to cry as she tried to put her hair back in place. While pressing the clumps of her hair onto her head she could feel the vile snakes. They were hideous and as she removed her hands the strands of yellow hair dropped to the ground. It was obvious that her hair was not going to go back. She flopped to the ground and began sobbing madly.

CHAPTER 5

Finally unable to cry anymore Medusa sat up. Sniffling from her now runny nose, she sighed. She had no idea what she should do now. An overwhelming desire to go home and hug her mother struck her but there was probably no way that her mother would want anything to do with her now. She was a hideous looking monster. Medusa was just confused. That man who claimed to be the God of the sea tried to take advantage of her. Instead of Athena protecting a virtuous worshipper she cursed Medusa. It made no sense. Maybe it was the practical side from her mother but Medusa immediately began to wonder what she should do now. Glancing back over at the massive statue of Athena she seethed with a sudden anger. All of those stories of the gods being kind and benevolent clearly were untrue. She saw her potted olive tree sitting on the pedestal. Suddenly her anger shifted towards herself. She put so much work into that tree and THIS was her reward. Medusa was a fool. She scurried to her feet and ran up to the pot.

Scooping it up she yelled, "You do not deserve this!"

Tossing the pot as hard as she could directly at the statue, the clay pot shattered and the dirt within the pot splashed into the gold of the chiton. The tree fell onto the pedestal. An overwhelming urge to escape this place struck her. No doubt she could not go home since they would likely attack her on sight. She had no idea where to go next. She had nothing. In a hurry to leave she wrapped her himation over her head to cover her now hideous face and as she approached the exit of the Parthenon she saw a large group of very well armed men walking through the Propylaea and heading directly towards her. Medusa panicked. Even with whatever Athena had done to her she was not ready to die. She turned around and ran as fast as she could in the other direction through the Parthenon. On the other side of the massive statue of Athena was a doorway heading out of the temple on the opposite side of where the men were approaching from. As she ran out of the door she realized immediately that she was in even more trouble. While circling around the large hill that the Parthenon sat on she forgot that the end she was on was set on what was almost a sharp cliff.

"Oh no, oh no, oh no." She said to herself in a panicked tone.

She started pacing from side to side as she got to the edge of Cecropia. The top part of it was neatly leveled and set in marble to allow worshipers to get a stunning view of Athens. Looking down she saw that the side of the cliff side was rough. It was a rocky incline that ended on a busy walkway below. It looked very unsafe, especially since she had never climbed anything in her life.

A loud booming male voice behind her called out, "Spread out and search for the monster. Do not look at it directly if you see it."

She could hear people in the Parthenon and if she did not find an escape route they would find her. There was no other way out, she decided that she had to try to climb down. Wrapping her himation firmly around her hideous head, making sure to tie the ends, she lifted her chiton up as she clambered over the side and turned slightly to try step backwards. She looked downwards and saw a slight lip to put her toes in. Slowly she lowered her foot down to the lip and set her foot on it. It seemed solid. Next she lowered her other foot onto the lip and then began to look for another spot to put a foot at. Both of her hands were now hanging off the ledge of the marble edge of the overlook off of the Cecropia. Nerves began to overcome her. She had no idea what she was doing but she knew that she had to get away. Looking back down she was unable to see another lip. Reaching out with her left leg, she moved downward and tapped several times before her foot landed on what seemed to be a firm spot. Carefully she shifted her weight to her left foot and then lowered her hands down to the lip that she was once standing on. Moving cautiously she set her right foot downwards hoping to find a safe spot to set it down.

Right as her foot finally found purchase in which to allow Medusa to settle her weight she heard a male voice above her but out of sight yelling out, "It is not out here Gennadios."

Medusa froze and tried to keep as quiet as possible. Listening while holding her breath she heard the man above her walk away. Lowing her right foot down again she moved to find another spot. Her foot made contact with a smoother spot. As she shifted to move her weight to her right foot, whatever she had that foot on gave way. Giving out a squeal she found herself hanging precariously with her two hands slipping as she struggled to regain her balance. She shifted and pulled while scrabbling to regain her hold on the lip. After a few scary moments she was able to get a firm grip once again. Both of her hands were starting to hurt while holding herself on the lip. After she got her balance back she started to work her way down the rocky cliff side. Moving with even more caution she continued climbing down the cliff side. At this point she was almost down to the walkway. Oddly enough there was a large crowd walking back and forth and yet none of them seemed to even notice her climbing along. As she made it safely to the ground she sighed heavily. Glancing upwards she spotted several of the men looking down from the Cecropia at the crowd she was in. Hoping that they did not see her she began walking away. She had no idea where to go since there was no doubt that her family would reject her for she had become. Assuming that they did not turn into stone by looking at her. So far every person who looked at her ugly face turned to stone. As she started walking down the pathway away from the Cecropia she kept her head down but glanced up enough to see where she was headed. Off in the distance she spotted her cousin and Euryale walking towards her. She panicked once again because she knew that Euryale would recognize her, even with her himation over her head. Spinning on her heel Medusa turned around and began walking as briskly as she could in the other direction. After taking about ten steps she spotted a large group of men with swords stopping everyone on the pathway examining each person quite closely. Medusa realized when she saw them that they were looking for her.

"Oh no." She mumbled to herself.

Panic struck her when she realized that she was trapped. Behind her was her sister and in front of her was these men. Glancing around her she spotted a nearby alleyway. It was her only avenue of escape. Moving as quickly as she could, she scurried into the alleyway and then turned around to hide behind a nearby outcropping from one of the buildings. Peeking out, she watched as her sister and cousin slowly walked closer to the men with swords.

One of the men stopped her cousin and sister before ordering, "Have her remove her himation."

"How dare you approach my cousin in this manner?" Demosthenes said angrily.

Euryale stepped backward and slightly behind him as he drew his sword.

"Calm yourself." The man told Demosthenes before continuing, "There was a monster attacking people in the Parthenon. We are searching for it right now."

"A monster?" Euryale asked nervously.

"Yes. A hideous beast with light green skin, snakes for hair, and sinister blue eyes."

Medusa was shocked by his description. She did not notice her skin was not the same. Glancing down she immediately realized that he was right. Her skin did appear to be a light yellowish-green color. She frowned.

"That sounds hideous." Demosthenes stated.

"Indeed. Its attack turned several priestesses to stone before disappearing. It is the size of a young woman so we are checking all young women."

Euryale removed her himation revealing her normal appearance.

“Carry on.” The man told her before he began to examine the next person.

Mournfully Medusa looked at Euryale. She wanted nothing more than to run up to her and hug her. Deep down inside she knew that Euryale would not only reject her but those around her would probably attack Medusa.

“Medusa?” Euryale asked very nervously.

“She was in the Parthenon. Let us go now!” Demosthenes declared urgently before turning and running down the path towards the Propylaea.

Euryale began running as well. They were out of sight in a matter of a brief moment. She realized that she needed to find something to cover her arms or else she would be found out quickly. Her himation was barely enough to cover her head, neck, and some of her shoulders. What she needed was a much longer himation, one probably made for an older woman or better yet a man. Where would she find one? She had no money and going back home to get one was not an option. Walking further down the alley, which was slightly darker due to the two marble buildings being closer together, she headed away from the Parthenon. As she walked along she spotted several swaths of cloth hanging off of the side of one of the homes. She frowned because she knew that she would have to take one in order to cover her arms. Slowing her pace to examine the cloth hanging from the wall she noticed that one of them was clearly a very large himation. It was dyed lightly with a blood wine red color with simple embroidery along one of the edges. Stealing was not something that she particularly wanted to do but what other option did she have? Maybe by exchanging her current himation with it would be better than just stealing it. Moving as cautiously as she could, she snuck over to the back area behind the home of where the clothing was hanging along a nearby wall. Peering around to make sure that no one was nearby she reached out and slipped the large himation hanging off the side of the wall of the building. She ripped off her own himation and wrapped this one around her head as fast as she could.

A voice called out through the wall of the building that she took the cloth from, "Who is stealing my himation!"

Turning away from the road that she came from, Medusa began to run. She made it a slight distance away before something struck her from behind, knocking her down.

"You little rat. I am going to beat you senseless." A very angry female voice yelled from behind Medusa.

Struggling to her feet Medusa felt something strike her back and force her down against the ground. A rock or something scraped a deep cut into her cheek. Her best guess was whatever hit her was a stick as it hit her back again. It hurt quite a bit. Finally able to scrabble to her feet Medusa took off running again. This time she was able to get away. She heard the woman's voice yelling at her but Medusa's hard breathing masked whatever the woman was saying. She kept running as fast as she could until she was unable to run. Medusa had no idea where in Athens she was when she stopped to try and catch her breath. It took her several moments to be able to breath normally again. She had not ran so much in a very long time. The left side of her chin hurt and when she touched it with her hand her hand became sticky with what she guessed was probably blood. Looking at her hand she was appalled to see that the blood on her hand was a light green color! Her hand started to shake uncontrollably. Her head began swimming from thoughts outside her ability to grasp. It made no sense to her why Athena did this to her. She slumped to the ground on her rear while staring at her hand covered in green blood.

CHAPTER 6

Medusa sat on the ground staring at her hand for some time before she heard someone walk nearby. Whoever it was kept walking but their presence knocked her out of her daze. Cautiously standing up, Medusa took a moment to look around to try and figure out where she was. She ran so hard and fast that she was not paying attention to the part of Athens that she had ran towards. The buildings around her were the sun-dried brick ones that she had spotted when she first arrived in Athens. It was clearly the poorest neighborhood of Athens. The smell of chamber pots was quite overwhelming. She started to wander aimlessly. There was no way that she could go back to Piraeus, it was not as though she knew of anyone who would take a hideous monster into their home. As she wandered, making sure to keep her head down and fully covered by her himation to not catch anyone's attention, she noticed dozens of small filthy children running around. Unlike most of Athens, which had stone pathways, this area was just dirt paths. She could hear the hustle and bustle of the crowd round her. Her stomach rumbled slightly. It had been some time since she last ate something. Giving a deep frown she glanced around. There was nothing that she could help herself to. After continuing to walk along for some time Medusa spotted a fig tree off on the side in someone's yard. Looking carefully she noticed that while there was a crowd around her, no one was looking at her. She moved briskly as she could towards the tree.

Lifting one of the corners of her himation she started picking off a few fresh figs.

As she reached up for another one she heard a female voice yell out, “Get away from my tree!”

Instead of looking to see who it was yelling, Medusa ran off down the walkway. She was not looking to get hit by another stick. After her mad dash she ran around a very old and beat up building. Once there she felt safe so she slumped down to her rear and greedily began eating the fig in her hand.

While eating a second fig a different younger female voice next to Medusa asked, “Hungry?”

Making sure not to reveal her face, Medusa looked at whoever was talking to her. It was a young girl with loose black hair, brown eyes, and dark tanned skin. Her chiton was very old looking and slightly dirty. Medusa guessed immediately that the girl was around ten years old. She was not wearing a himation or any other head covering. Medusa had heard tales of the poorest of Athens not living up to the standards of a traditional Athenian woman.

“Yes.” She told the girl before taking another bite of the fig she had stolen.

The girl chuckled before stating, “You are going to starve to death while being chased off trying to get figs.”

Taking another bite Medusa sullenly replied, “It is all I have.”

“Join the club. Half of us here have nothing, you do not have to starve though.”

“What do you mean?” Medusa asked curiously.

Giving out a giggle the girl stated, “You are new here.”

Almost defensively Medusa replied, “It is none of your business.”

The girl laughed at Medusa before declaring, “Yes. Very new here. Well, I am going to give you some free advice. Do not wander at night, hide somewhere and stay there. The slave hunters go out looking for girls like us to turn into slaves.”

She stood up and jogged way. Medusa frowned. From the daughter of a scribe to a homeless fugitive. No doubt the men chasing her back on the Parthenon would continue looking for her and if these slave hunters ran into her it would only help them. She went back to finishing the stolen figs. They were the best tasting figs that she had ever eaten in her life. Slowly standing up she glanced around carefully once again. There was a few dozen very poor looking people moving about her minding their own business. The women were walking openly without a male escort, their skin much darker and more tanned, and the children running freely while playing without supervision. Her mother never let Medusa or her sisters run free, she always said it was unbecoming of a woman and unsafe as well.

Medusa frowned thinking about it as she mumbled to herself, "She was right."

It almost burned to acknowledge that her mother was right. Medusa and her sisters heard her mother constantly deflect their desire to go outside with claims of how dangerous it was outside of their home alone. Medusa was now living proof that her mother was right. Giving out a deep sigh she looked around yet again. There was still a crowd of poor Athenians moving around her and thankfully outside of the young girl who just spoke to her, no one had taken any notice of Medusa. It was well past noon and she had no idea what she would do for supper or even more importantly, sleep. She started to walk aimlessly around the poor neighborhood. No one seemed to care or notice her. It was a bit of time while wandering before hunger hit her again. There was nothing open or available that she could see for her to eat. Her stomach started to hurt from hunger. She frowned deeply once she realized that not only was she going to have to go to bed without food but also have to sleep on the street. The sun was fully setting as Medusa just gave up and wandered over to a beat up looking home that was resting slightly away from the main pathway. Sighing heavily she flopped down onto the ground next to the rough wooden door of the home. There was no light coming out of the building and she suspected that whoever lived there was probably asleep. She doubted that they would complain about her resting up against the wall of the outside of the home, especially if she woke up early in the morning and left before they woke up.

Her eyelids started to get heavy as she began to drift off to sleep before suddenly someone violently yanked on her arm closest to the door of the building. She squeaked out in fear.

A slightly familiar female voice from the door whispered out, "Are you daft? I told you not to stay out at night."

Medusa looked over at the person speaking and saw the girl who approached her earlier in the day about the figs. She was kneeling as she reached through the open door to pull on Medusa's arm.

"Where can I go?" Medusa asked huffily.

"Get in." The girl gestured towards her door.

Having nowhere else to go Medusa shuffled to her feet and entered through the door. She heard the door close behind her along with a grinding noise of something being pushed up against the door. Glancing around Medusa could see little in the room but as her eyes adjusted she realized that the unlit room was barren of any furniture and quite beat up.

The girl whispered, "Get down and lean against these crates."

Medusa turned to look at her and saw the girl, along with three other girls, where leaning against the crate. Medusa was very confused by why they were doing that.

The girl repeated but this time more huffily in a whispered tone, "Get down and lean against these crates!"

Kneeling down Medusa leaned against the crates with the others. She was still very confused. Taking a moment to look at the other girls Medusa guessed that they were all slightly younger than she was and just as homeless. Each was wearing dirty and worn chitons, without a himation, and looked like they direly need a bath. They all seemed very scared and were putting all of their weight into the crate up against the door.

Suddenly she could hear a gruff but younger male voice through the walls of the building call out, "I swear, I saw a girl out here. Fan out and search for her. The Lokhagos needs more young girls to sell. And make sure to be gentle with them and Cleonicus keep your hands off them, we need untouched women because they are worth more."

"I did not…" Another voice angrily retorted but he was interrupted by the first voice.

"Yes you did and it took everything I could muster to keep the Lokhagos from having you tossed head first into the ocean off a cliff. Now go find that girl."

There was a dead silence before a pair of footsteps approached the door of the building that Medusa and the girls were in. The girls around her tensed up and began actively pushing against the crate. She felt an urge to push now that she realized what was going on so she began pushing as hard as she could.

The footsteps stopped and a voice said, "Pentheus this old building was home to some hag for a while. Should I check in here?"

Her heart was beating madly

"Of course Cleonicus you idiot." The original voice replied.

Medusa pushed against the crate as hard as she could when she heard the man pushing against the door.

Thankfully between the five girls they were able to keep the door from budging and it was obvious the man was fooled when he called out, "It will not open Pantheus."

"Then it is probably locked you fool. Move on to the next door."

Medusa sighed in relief. Things could have gotten very messy if the men hunting for her managed to get into the home. She sat quietly with the other girls until the sound of the men searching for them seemed to have gone.

The girl Medusa who ran into earlier whispered, "We got lucky that time. They got Theophania two nights ago and if we are not careful they will get any one of us next."

"What in the world are they chasing us for?" Medusa asked curiously.

Two of the girls grumbled something that she could not hear.

"Are you daft? They clearly want to turn us into some sort of slave for rich people. Most likely to have their way with us and toss us to the wolves." The girl who pulled Medusa into the home huffily whispered.

"Oh." Was all Medusa could say.

She did not fully understand just how much trouble she was in during that brief moment. This was not the life that she wanted to lead, one of a homeless girl being hunted and on the run, but she had no idea where the heck or what the heck to do with herself.

The girl who had initially met Medusa stood and announced, "Well I guess we should get some sleep. This home used to belong to an old woman who died without a family. No one claimed it so we use it to hide in regularly."

Looking over at Medusa the girl said, "My name is Agnodice."

One of the other girls whispered, "I am Phoebe."

Another declared, "Sotera."

"Zoe." The youngest looking one announced.

Finally the last one stated, "And I am Pasiphae."

The girl who said she was Agnodice asked, "So, what is your name?"

Seeing nothing dangerous about being honest with her name Medusa told them, "I am Medusa."

"Never heard that name before." A girl who Medusa believed called herself Pasiphae.

It was hard to see so Medusa was not entirely who was who.

Not sure how to respond Medusa told her, "I do not know where my mother got it."

"Oooo, one of us actually has a mother. What did she do? Abandon you?" Another of the girls asked.

Agnodice snipped, "Stop. It does not matter how we all got here. All that matters is surviving. All of you get some sleep. Rest up against the crates in case those bastards come back."

None of the other girls said a word before laying down against all sides of the crate that was resting against the door. It was quite clear to Medusa that Agnodice was the leader of this little band. Also, it was obvious to Medusa that she could not hide in Athens for very long but she had no idea where to go and no idea how to get there. She was totally lost.

Agnodice sat down next to her and whispered, "Get some sleep. We have a busy day tomorrow as I am going to show you the ropes."

Giving Agnodice a nod Medusa settled down onto the dirt floor. All of the excitement caused her to forget that she was hungry. Now laying there trying to sleep her stomach grumbled madly. There was nothing she could do about it so she closed her eyes. After a bit of a struggle she was finally able to get some sleep.

CHAPTER 7

The sound of people walking outside of the home that Medusa was now sleeping in caused her to wake. Her body was quite sore from sleeping on a floor and her stomach roared in hunger. She rolled over slowly before sitting up. The other girls were soundly sleeping still. After finding a chamber pot, she washed her hands in an old basin sitting in one of the back rooms. The small home was barely furnished. All signs led her to believe that someone might have pillaged anything of value that was once there. Medusa was just glad that the chamber pot and a wash basin were still there. She wagered that Agnodice and her friends might have likely brought them into the empty room.

As Medusa reentered the small main area of the building Agnodice said, "I see you are awake."

"Yes."

Agnodice stood up and as she walked up to Medusa she instructed, "Come with me."

Confused by what she wanted Medusa followed her through the small home to the one bedroom near the back of it.

"I am not going to ask what happened or where you came from but before we can let you join us I need to know why your skin seems so sickly. Do you have something others can catch?"

Almost on instinct she tucked her hands underneath the large himation that she had over herself. Thinking about it she doubted that anyone could catch what she guessed was a curse from Athena. She frowned. Even trying to hide her skin it was still clear that she was different. There was no way that she could hide the entirety of her skin all the time.

Finally she told Agnodice, “No.”

She did not want to say anything, and most certainly did not want to explain exactly what was wrong with her. No doubt if Agnodice or the other girls saw the hideous monster that Medusa was they would flee, assuming they did not turn into stone like everyone else that saw her now hideous face.

“Fine. Today we will show you how to get food so you do not starve to death.”

Medusa was very curious so she asked, “How do you do it?”

“We sometimes go to richer areas and beg until we are chased off. We borrow sometimes.”

Interrupting her Medusa asked, “Borrow?”

“Steal. We steal food to eat.”

Medusa was not over happy about the idea of stealing but she realized that she was not in the position to be the woman of high morals that she was raised to be.

“The others are awake. Let us go.” Agnodice instructed.

Medusa followed her out of the small room and into the main area where the others were standing. Now she was able to see all of them more clearly. Each looked like a typical Athenian girl except they were much thinner than most Medusa had seen before. Their clothing was bedraggled and dirty.

Agnodice announced, “Today we will try our luck again in the Agora.”

The girl that Medusa remembered was named Sotera asked, “Will they just kick us out again?”

“If we start with the begging. Today we are going to take food. Since Medusa is dressed so much nicer than the rest of us she can distract vendors enough for one of us to get something.”

Medusa did not like being used as bait but she realized that the plan was probably the best way to go. She simply nodded at Agnodice’s announcement. The other girls said nothing and followed as Agnodice led them out of the home carefully. Medusa stopped to look around for a moment and noticed a group of men hovering around examining the crowd. None of them looked familiar to her. She continued walking with the other girls as they headed to the Agora. Medusa had walked through the outskirts of it while heading to the Acropolis when she arrived in Athens. Reflecting on everything, she regretting coming to honor Athena. Based just on how Athena acted when Medusa was being attacked, she was unworthy of the honor that Medusa was trying to give her. In fact she found herself detesting Athena. Why would the gods treat their worshipers this way? She frowned heavily thinking about it.

As they walked along Agnodice announced, “I think we should have Zoe and Pasiphae pretend to be slave girls for Medusa. Medusa will act like one of the rich girls walking around shopping. She can distract vendors in the Agora while Phoebe and Sotera cover for me as I get us some food.”

The girls with Agnodice said nothing so Medusa just nodded. Her mind wandered as she tried to think of what to say. She had never been to a market before, least yet bought something from someone. As they continued to walk the crowd around them got thicker with mostly men moving around. She did however spot the occasional women and a few girls. As they moved along Agnodice gestured towards a cart that was lined near the outskirts of the Agora, with the back of the cart facing down an alley. Medusa could see why Agnodice chose it. The three girls should be able to sneak up pretty easily and make an escape just as easily.

Agnodice approached Medusa and whispered, “Do you know what to do?”

“No.” Medusa replied honestly.

“You just need to distract the trader while we sneak up and get some food. All we need is a few things.”

Medusa nodded at her. She was a bit nervous but her stomach was rumbling madly. In all of her entire life she had never gone this long without eating something. While she did not eat large amounts of food, like her father and brother, she did eat regular meals. Swallowing down her nerves she strode towards the trader. Checking her himation, which still covered all of her head and shoulders, she adjusted her arms a bit to hide them fully. Her hands were still slightly exposed so she grabbed a hold of the edges of her himation to keep it in place while hiding her hands. Zoe and Pasiphae would be pretending to be her slaves so she did not need to hold or touch anything.

Before moving Agnodice declared, "Wait until you see us near the back of the trader's table before you walk up. Medusa you do not say or do anything except stand back. Zoe and Pasiphae will do all the talking for you. Just keep walking and standing like you normally do."

Zoe sarcastically interjected, "All rich like."

The others all giggled in response. Medusa said nothing because she did not really think how she stood was very different. She took a moment to look at the other girls at it hit her. They all slouched excessively, although Agnodice did so the least.

"Alright enough games. I am hungry." Agnodice ordered.

Watching carefully Medusa observed Agnodice and the two other girls leave the Agora. After a bit of a wait she spotted them approaching the side alley.

"Okay," Zoe stated, "We should walk around looking for a while before heading to the one that we are heading to. Just stand kind of behind us and watch us carefully."

Medusa replied, "Alright."

They slowly moved from table to table. After a few moments they finally arrived at the one that Agnodice chose as a target. As they approached the table Zoe picked up an apricot spoke to the trader. It was an older man wearing an older chiton and simple leather sandals. His shock white hair was balding and he had a longer scraggly white beard. There was no doubt this men stayed outside every day as his skin was heavily tanned. Medusa glanced around examining the large crowd surrounding them but kept an eye out for Agnodice. She finally spotted Agnodice stealthily approaching from behind the trader's table. Zoe and Pasiphae started haggling with the man. Medusa could actually see glee in the man's eye as they argued about pricing. Agnodice disappeared behind the man and Medusa lost track of what she was doing. After a few nervous moments she reappeared and then stealthily snuck away. Zoe glanced back at Medusa and nodded at her.

Using the opportunity to help them escape the argument Medusa stated sternly, "Enough, I wish to leave."

Zoe set down the apricot she was holding and walked away with Pasiphae shuffling behind her. Medusa followed them. After walking back out of the Agora they spotted Agnodice, Phobe, and Sotera standing nearby. Phobe and Sotera looked very happy. Once Medusa got close enough she could see why. Agnodice was holding up the loose end of her chiton and within it was not just some fruit by several pieces of dried fish. Medusa's stomach grumbled at the sight of it all.

Grinning at them Agnodice stated, "Let us get out of here before that trader realizes what happened."

They strolled along for a little while before Agnodice led them into a small park. It was not very popular for some unknown reason. Medusa thought it was quite pretty with open grass and a few statues of some of the gods. She scowled when she spotted Athena.

"Okay it is time to eat." Agnodice announced.

Medusa shrugged off her anger before sitting down between Zoe and Sotera. Agnodice passed out several apricots, apples, and gave each of them a piece of dried fish. That boring unflavored dried fish was probably the best thing that Medusa had ever ate in her life. She gobbled it down before taking a bite out of the apricot. It was fresh and sweet. Once she finished all of her food she felt much better.

"Let us do it again." Agnodice announced.

The other girls agreed. They all walked back and repeated the same process again, this time on the opposite side of the Agora and far away from the first trader that they stole from. This time they got some dried meat and a few fresh vegetables. After splitting up the food Medusa found herself full.

Agnodice stated, "We should not push our luck anymore. I think I want to give Medusa a tour of our neighborhood."

The four other girls gave their verbal agreement before leaving the pair alone.

Once they were gone Agnodice asked, "Where are you from?"

Seeing no harm in answering Medusa answered, "Piraeus."

"How did you end up here?"

"I really do not want to talk about it."

Agnodice nodded thoughtfully and after a long pause she stated, "Okay. Let me show you our neighborhood. I know it is not the best but it is all we have. We get chased out of most of Athens."

"Why?"

"They do not want people begging near their nice shiny marble buildings."

"Oh."

Agnodice nodded before declaring, "We are the lost and unwanted. The only people who look for us are the slavers."

"Is there any way to deal with them?"

Agnodice laughed before declaring, "Most of them are in the military and the leaders are nobles. They control Athens and we are trash."

"Oh."

"I know. Well, how about I show you the neighborhood?"

"Alright."

Medusa walked behind Agnodice as she walked through the poorest neighborhood in Athens.

Agnodice pointing at a well before stating, "This is the main well in the neighborhood. You can use it to get water. We keep a few buckets in the house we moved into but make sure that you are careful when you do it. During the day we are safe but in at night is when we need to be hiding. We also found a small cave near the outskirts of Athens nearby that we hide in sometimes, just to change our pattern."

Medusa had to admit that her plan made sense. If they were being hunted it would be wise to move around occasionally. They continued walking with Agnodice introducing her to a few others who were known to help the needy in Athens. These people at times would offer old used clothing, especially younger people like Agnodice and Medusa. They walked through the dirty old neighborhood for a while before Agnodice brought Medusa to a rough park. The park was lined with beat-up statues that had not been maintained in some time.

Agnodice stated, "A long time ago this neighborhood used to be one of the best neighborhoods in Athens. Over time better ones were built while no one did anything here. These statues were apparently some of the most beautiful statues in Athens. Now they are half broken down with any piece of gold once on them long stolen."

They sat there chatting about nothing in particular before Agnodice decided it was time to walk around more. Medusa was growing to appreciate Athens as they strolled along. They left the small neighborhood that they were in and walked through some of the wealthier parts. She even recognized one as the area where she would have ended up had she not been cursed and was married. She sighed heavily. There was nothing that she could think of to do to change her fate. She was just a dumb girl from a small town outside of Athens. It would take a miracle to fix her problem. It suddenly dawned on her that maybe she could find someone wise enough to help cure her. Her mind wandered thinking about the stories her mother had told her. The only one that popped into her mind who might have been useful was the Oracle of Delphi. She had no idea where it was or how to get there. It was something she would have to inquire about it.

Casually attempting to learn more Medusa asked, "Do you know anything about Delphi?"

Agnodice must not have realized Medusa's intent because she answered, "Yes. It is a small city northwest of hear. Not much there other than Apollo worshipers and the Oracle."

"How far is it from here?"

Raising an eyebrow Agnodice turned to look at Medusa before asking, "Why you planning to go see the Oracle? No one goes there without going through a journey. They are heavily fortified."

Awkwardly trying not to reveal her position Medusa mumbled out, "No, I was just curious."

Agnodice laughed uproariously before declaring, "You are the worst liar. You do not need to be ashamed of your plans. You must first travel there and request an audience. The Priestesses will instruct you."

Deciding to not try to lie further Medusa asked, "How far is it from here?"

"Taking rest regularly every day it is probably about a few days walk away from Athens. That is all I know."

Medusa nodded at her. They walked along for a bit longer before finding their way back to the others. The sun was starting to set as the girls all went into the small home they had occupied the night before. Medusa was quite happy that they already had food. They had stolen enough for the next day as well and stored all of it in the home that they were in. After eating dinner they laid down with the door blocked by a crate and slept.

CHAPTER 8

Medusa was startled awake by the sound of something banging against the door. She realized immediately that it was the men who were chasing them last night.

A voice that seemed familiar from last night penetrated through the door, "I saw them go in there. I have been watching them since this morning. They are in there."

"Right Cleonicus. Take Andronikos around the back and we will find out soon enough."

Agnodice's panicked voice whispered out, "Everyone hide. Use the crates against the back wall."

She moved quickly and quietly towards one of the big crates. Before anyone could make a further move the front door slammed open as one very large brutish man slammed through. He had loose long hair just down to his shoulders and a scruffy beard that appeared to just be starting to grow. The only clothing he had on was a simple off-white chiton and a pair of leather sandals. In his left hand was a torch, which lit the room up fully. A belt was tied around his waist and it held both a coin pouch and a sheathed sword. As he stumbled over the crate that once blocked the door two other men followed in behind him. They were dressed the same and appeared to be young men, Medusa guessed that they were around the same age as her one time future fiancée. They wore the same clothing with a sword and coin pouch as well.

"Ha!" The voice that Medusa recognized as the leader of the group called out, "We found a jackpot of fresh young slaves.

Agnodice called out, “Run!”

The girls started to move towards the back door but almost immediately another pair of men appeared through the door that the girls were heading towards. Medusa, who was in the corner of the room away from the door, was totally frozen in panic.

The leader of the men ordered, “Collect them all.”

After a pause he bellowed out, “Carefully.”

Medusa backed into the corner away from the men, completely trapped. She had no idea how the heck she was going to escape. The other girls began to scream out in panic as the much larger men swarmed on them.

The leader of the men stepped directly towards Medusa and declared, “I will get this one.”

She was overwhelmed with fear as she looked to the left and right trying to find a way to escape. There was nothing. She spotted Agnodice cornered while swinging her fists and feet wildly at one of the men. He was obviously not expecting such a fight due to his facial expression. All of the other girls were partially subdued. The man reached out to grab Medusa and she attempted to flee away from him. He grabbed her himation, which spun loose as she tried to slip from his grasp. She spun to look back at him and he froze in fear from her appearance.

He muttered out the words, “By the…” before he turned quickly into a statue made of stone.

A voice called out, “A monster!”

Medusa looked at him and he too froze before turning to stone. She reached out to grab her himation from statue of the one-time man in front of her. As she wrapped it around her head she looked around. She was stunned to see that everyone in the room, excluding Agnodice, were now statues made of stone. Even the girls, most of which were now statues within the hands of the men who captured them, were stone. Agnodice’s facial expression was a mixture of fear and shock. It was now that it dawned on Medusa how her curse worked. The only ones who would turn to stone are the ones who looked directly into her eyes. Agnodice was the only one who was not looking at her when the man removed her himation. It was because Agnodice was busy trying to fend off the man attempting to capture her.

"What in Hades are you?" Agnodice asked.

"I am a girl from Piraeus who was cursed."

Agnodice's face shifted to obvious curiosity as she asked, "Cursed?"

Medusa nodded at her.

"How?"

Letting out a deep sad sigh Medusa paused briefly before finally answering, "I was trying to offer a small olive tree to Athena when a man attempted to rape me at her temple. Athena must have thought we were lovers, although he was a disgusting old man and I am young, because she appeared and declared a curse on me. The man transformed into Poseidon and laughed before leaving. She left with him and kept me cursed."

"That does not seem right."

Medusa paused yet again before sighing.

After another pause she declared, "It was not fair and now I am a hideous monster."

"And Delphi?"

"I was thinking that the Oracle of all beings would know how to lift this curse."

Agnodice paused for a long moment thinking. She even rubbed her chin softly before her facial expression shifted. It was clear to Medusa that she came up with an idea.

Reaching out to grab the coin purse on the man who was trying to capture her she declared, "Well, I guess now you have the funds to get there. There are five of these bastards and I am certain they come from wealthy families. No doubt they carry plenty of coin on them. You take three and I will take two."

"And what will you do?"

Agnodice turned towards another of the men before declaring, "I need to get out of here. I think I will head to Egypt, I heard they respect women. They even let them practice medicine."

Medusa gave her a nod.

As she reached out to grab a second coin pouch Agnodice announced, “It will not be long until someone realizes that these bastards are missing. If I were you I would get out of Athens now.”

Once she had a hold of the second coin pouch she strolled by the door that the men knocked down.

Turning back to Medusa she stated, “Good luck Medusa. I hope you find what you are looking for.”

Agnodice disappeared into the night. Medusa glanced around to look at the various statues in the room. All of them had facial expressions of either horror or shock. It dawned on her that while she was a monster now, this curse could be useful in emergencies. She removed the first coin purse and opened it. She was stunned to see a pair of silver didrachm, a few drachma, and an obol. While she knew it was nowhere near the amount of money her father had, this alone should be enough to get her to Delphi. The other two coin purses had a little less than the amount of coin as the one from the men’s leader but they added significant value to her ability to move freely.

She was still very tired and there was no way she could stay in this building so she muttered to herself, “I guess I should get to walking, I can sleep later.”

Medusa had not noticed it when the men first entered but one of them had some sort of bag hanging off of his shoulder and tied in place by a rope. She realized that she could probably use some supplies so she carefully removed the bag from his stone arm and opened it. The bag was empty, which was disappointing, but she got the bag at least. She decided to take the chiton and sheathed sword off of the smallest of the five men. Even though she had no idea how to use a sword she decided that it might be useful so she tucked it into the bag. Finally she collected up the last of the food from earlier in the day. She strolled out of the home and began walking towards where she knew the northern pathway of Athens would be. After she got closer to the edges of Athens she spotted a group of soldiers guarding the path into Athens.

Deciding that she would need basic direction to Delphi she walked up to the group of men and asked, “Excuse me, could you tell me which path leads to Delphi?”

The men looked initially confused, which she guessed was because she was a young woman out at dark.

One of them recovered after a brief moment before stating, “It is that way.”

“Thank you.” Medusa told him before starting off along the road that the man pointed towards.

She could hear them talking to each other but she could not hear what they were saying. No doubt it was more than a little surprise. She did not care. At this point she had realized that all she would have to do is take off her himation and look at them. They would be turned to stone. She did not want to do that to people but she would defend herself. After some time walking she started to get quite tired. She knew that she would need some sleep very soon. There was nothing around her off the pathway but rough rocky hillside and plenty of shrubs. She decided that she could move off the roadway a bit and sleep in some bushes out of sight. Stopping to make sure no one was following her she moved up a hillside and into some bushes that were nestled against a small outcropping. As she sat down quietly she was surprised when a group of men came into view. She recognized them immediately as some of the men who were at the outskirts of Athens. The one she had asked for directions was leading them and carrying a torch. They followed her! She was disgusted. Where there no noble men in Athens? It seemed as though they were all out to ruin others for their own gain. Sitting as quietly as possible she watched the men as they continued out of sight down the road. It was probably a good thing that she planned to sleep since she was now trapped there some time. Moving as slowly and quietly as possible she laid down while setting herself up to watch the path. While lying there eventually her eyes started to get entirely too heavy and she found herself drifting off to sleep.

* * * * *

Medusa's eyes flickered open to the early morning sunrise. She felt much better after some sleep. Glancing at the pathway she saw no one in sight. No doubt the men who were after her gave up after a bit of time and headed back to Athens. She pulled herself out of the bushes and as she walked down the hillside she dusted off the bits of leaves that had stuck to her. It was a very long walk to Delphi but what other choice did she have? She was a hideous monster. Even she knew that the Oracle of Delphi was the wisest being alive. If anyone would know how to lift this curse it would be the Oracle. Glancing into her bag she pulled out some dried fish and ate it. Her stomach was rumbling and the amount of food that she had would not last very long. The first thing she thought of was if there was a chance of running into a village where she could buy more food. The weather was pleasant enough and the pathway was empty so Medusa kept plugging along. It was almost lunch time when she finally spotted what appeared to be a small village off in the distance on the path that she was on. She was quite pleased to see it. After a bit more walking she slowly dragged her way into the new village. There was a sign as she entered that read 'Eleusis'. The village was nestled up against a large body of water and very much reminded her of her home in Piraeus. Her stomach was rumbling like mad and she moved quickly to find something to eat. Eleusis was a lot smaller than Piraeus and seemed very ramshackle in comparison. There was maybe twenty or so buildings, most of which appeared to just be homes. She spotted the small marketplace off in the distance. As she approached it she noticed that women out in the open was much more common, much like the poorer parts of Athens. It was dawning on her that the rules for women in Athens was only for those with money.

Moving to the nearest small table filled with fruits Medusa asked the older woman, "How much for some grapes and an apple?"

"An obol for all of it."

Medusa pulled out a silver obol and traded the fruit for it. She gobbled down the fruit and then bought a piece of baked lamb. Once she ate that she bought more fruit and dried fish to eat later. She was unsure when the next time that she would find another village. The idea to buy a blanket or two hit her. It might get cold at night as she moved closer to Delphi. After buying two wool blankets, which she folded and put in her bag, she started walking again. As she got to the end of the village heading towards Delphi she confirmed with the one guard that she was heading the right way before continuing. She was unsure how far it was but Agnodice mentioned a few days so she had to keep going. As she continued along, the coast line disappeared and everything around her started to get rockier. The pathway that she was on got very narrow, maybe just wide enough for a pair of horses at most. It was obviously a less popular path since she rarely ran into people walking along. She did see a small group of what she guessed were merchants but they did not even seem surprised to see a young woman walking alone on the pathway. Medusa's feet hurt so she had to stop and rest several times. As she continued along the sun began to set and her stomach was once again rumbling. She decided to only eat some of her food and save the rest for tomorrow. After eating she began walking again in the dark. It was almost impossible to see so she decided that she needed to get some rest. After shuffling along near the side of the pathway she found a small crevasse that was pretty smooth and out of sight. She pulled out one of the wool blankets and set it down to give her a little comfort before pulling out the second blanket and lying down. The chirping insects around her helped slowly put her to sleep.

* * * * *

The sound of several animals clomping along the pathway that was just out of sight woke Medusa from her sleep. She slowly peeked out of the crevasse to see a small caravan moving away from Athens. Once they fully cleared past her she collected up all of her blankets, which she folded and put back in her bag. Stepping carefully she walked out onto the pathway. She looked down the road to where the caravan was heading. It was still in sight but far enough way that they could not see her. She started to follow behind them. After walking for a bit in the morning she was able to spot what looking like a wide field with farms on it. The caravan continued along before finally another village came into view. This village was named 'Platea' and it was very basic just like the previous village that she had been to. She restocked all of her supplies, making sure to get more food, before continuing on. Once again she made sure to verify the direction that she was heading was the right one. After another two long days of walking Medusa finally found her way to Delphi. The city itself was nowhere near as large as Athens but it was just as shiny with bright white marble glistening against the mountainside. Medusa asked a guard for directions to the Oracle and was guided to a path that headed up a mountainside. Between two large mountains she spotted a walled temple. She headed up the path and oddly enough as she approached the walls she was surprised to see a young woman wearing a simple white chiton waiting for her. Her hair was neatly braided back into a bun and she looked very pretty.

As Medusa approached her the woman stated, "The Oracle is expecting you."

CHAPTER 9

Medusa was completely surprised by the declaration from who she guessed was a priestess. The most obvious question was how would the Oracle know who she is or why she was coming? Maybe the stories about this Oracle were true. Medusa sullenly nodded at her.

"Follow me." The woman ordered.

Medusa started following her as the woman turned away and started walking towards an opening in the walls around the temple where she believed that the Oracle lived. Even after visiting Athena's temple so recently Medusa found herself impressed by the temple of Apollo. It was a massive building with tall white pillars that opened up into the temple. She could see a beautifully painted wall just past the pillars. Her first guess that the Oracle was located inside the temple. She was proven right as the priestess guided her around the side of the temple and into the singular entrance in the front. The room that was the center of the temple was poorly lit and she struggled to see much. In fact she could really only see the candles around her and a heavy smoke. She had no idea where the smoke was coming from. The smoke did have an unusual wooden smell to it.

A female voice from in front of her but in the darkness said, "Leave us."

Medusa tried her best to see who was talking in the darkness but the limited candle light made it impossible. She started to take a step forward.

“Stay there.” The voice instructed firmly.

After she stopped walking Medusa asked, “You know who I am?”

“I do. I am the High Priestess of Apollo, more commonly known as the Oracle of Delphi. You are a woman cursed and you have questions.”

“I do, is there a cure?”

“First let me see you.”

“What?”

The voice instructed, “Remove your himation.”

“It is not safe.”

“As long as you cannot look into my eyes I will be unharmed. I wish to see if my vision was true.”

Medusa shrugged before removing her himation. At this point she had gotten so used to the hair of snakes that she just could ignore their occasional hissing. They responded to the himation being removed by hissing loudly as they flailed about. She thought that they did the same thing when the man had removed her himation a few days ago but she was quite distracted so she did not notice it.

“Oh yes,” The voice stated excitedly before continuing, “It is exactly as I foresaw it.”

Medusa was quite frustrated so she demanded to have her question answered, “Can the curse be lifted?”

“No. Once the gods curse you only that god can remove it.”

Medusa frowned because she knew that the cruel goddess Athena would not remove a curse, assuming she could even contact her.

“I know you are upset but everything serves a purpose.”

Anger flushed through her. Medusa was wrongly cursed and this person in the shadows was telling her that being cursed as some hideous monster served a ‘purpose’.

“Calm yourself, anger serves no purpose here.”

“And what is the purpose of me being cursed into this hideous monster.”

“I am not all knowing but I do know where you must go next.”

Medusa laughed. She had no clue what to do with herself and yet the Oracle hidden in the shadows claimed to know from just one meeting.

Grumpily she asked, “And where is that?”

“You must travel to the island of Kefalonia.”

Medusa frowned. She had heard of the island from some of the many conversations she spied upon that her father had with his friends. Kefalonia was best known for its wine if she remembered correctly. Her father loved Kefalonian wine. Everything else about the island was an unknown to her.

“Why there?” Medusa asked with a confused tone.

“It is all I know. Not all visions are clear and the only clear path I see takes you to Kefalonia. Now go. You must go to Cirrha and sail to Sami. From there I lose track of your fate.”

Seeing no other choice Medusa sighed heavily. Being in Athens or being in Kefalonia would not matter since she was now a monster who would scare away anyone who saw her, assuming they did not turn to stone first. She wrapped her himation back around her head, noticing as she did so that it was now pretty dingy looking, before turning and walking towards the exit.

The voice of the Oracle called out through the dark, “Good luck Medusa.”

As Medusa left one of the priestesses approached her and said, “The Oracle ordered us to provide you with some fresh clothing and a bath before you leave for Cirrha. Follow me and I will guide you to a private spot to bathe.”

Smiling to herself, she appreciated the small kindness. She knew that she was in dire need of a bath and change of clothing. Even this newer himation was getting very smelly from how she had to wear it. The priestess brought Medusa to a small white marble building that was nothing more than a room with a metal bath tub.

“I wish you luck. To get to Cirrha all you need to do is go down the pathway you came up and then follow the main road away from Athens and you will arrive in Cirrha in a short time. From there you head to the dock and simply hire a ship to Kefalonia.”

“Thank you.” Medusa told her right before the priestess turned and left.

Examining the small room she slipped off the himation around her head. Sitting on the stand next to the tub was a small stand that had a pile of neatly folded clothing. They looked very basic but Medusa was happy to wear something clean. She bathed and slipped on the new clothing. It was just a plain undyed chiton and long himation but she quickly packed up her old clothing into the bag before heading out. It really was a good thing that she had the himation wrapped around her head, there would be no way that the entire temple of people would not panic if they saw her. The interaction with the Oracle was very unusual. Medusa was surprised by her cool reaction to seeing what kind of monster Medusa was. It made her think that the Oracle had seen much worse. Once she was ready she strolled out of the bathroom. It was still mid-day so she decided to go ahead and head off to Cirrha. Double checking her new himation, making sure it was covering as much of her skin as she could, she started to walk. The port town named Cirrha was exactly as far away as the Oracle said it was. The town was a bit of a surprise as it was almost more of a fort than a normal town. It had a large wall around it with massive rectangular towers. As she entered she spotted the port, which consisted of five long piers for ships. She suspected this village had plenty of strangers coming and going because no one seemed to react to her at all. Since she had no idea how far the trip to Kefalonia was from here she stopped at the small marketplace to buy more food for her bag. Once she finished she headed to the port. Hopefully she could find someone to take her to Kefalonia. After bouncing from ship to ship she found a group that was heading there tomorrow morning. She decided to get a good night’s sleep in a bed so she hunted down a room to sleep. That took her a little time and before long she was able to finally sleep normally.

* * * * *

Medusa woke the next morning and quickly wrapped a himation over her head. She was still unhappy about what was going on but at least she felt as though she had regained control of her situation. If the Oracle said she needed to be on Kefalonia then there must have been an excellent reason for her to be there. She walked through the crowd that appeared out of nowhere. Last night the town was dead but now it was bustling. She was able to blend right into the crowd as she headed towards the dock that she hired a ride to her destination. The man who she hired was older with heavily worn skin and a balding hairline. His crew was only a small handful of men that looked very poor and ragged.

As she approached the smaller ship the old man said, "There is our passenger. We'll head off once everyone is aboard."

Medusa crossed over the wooden plank that rested between the ship and the dock before sitting down in an open chair near the back of the ship. Once she sat a pair of men used some long sticks to push the ship away from the dock before setting down the sticks and settling down to row. After a bit they stopped rowing when the ship seemed to move on its own. It took her a bit to realize it but the reason it was moving was wind pushing the large swath of square shaped cloth that was hanging off a piece of timber in the middle of the ship. She had never been on the water before and it was quite a bit of fun. Glancing backwards she examined the town that she left from. It was quickly becoming smaller and smaller. She had never seen anything like it in her life. Once the town finally disappeared from view she turned back around and looked forward. There was nothing but water in front of her. On both sides she could see specks of land off in the distance. This trip cost her a silver didrachm. The ride continued some time and as lunch time hit she got something from her bag to eat before turning back to enjoy herself. As she sat there enjoying the view she heard several of the men who were running the ship arguing with the old man who she hired. Turning to look at them she saw one of them point at her for a moment. From where they were she could not hear what they were saying over the snappy noise of the cloth pulling the ship and the water splashing against the side.

Focusing she heard one of them speak a little louder, "Why are we doing this for an obol when she paid you a didrachm?"

"It is my ship that's why?"

The men around the man she hired did not seem to like his answer. She was not involved in whatever was going on but she was becoming very concerned. All she wanted was a safe ride to Kefalonia.

"Not anymore." The man who was wearing a beat up looking chiton and was much larger than most of the others said loudly.

As the old man started to reply the other man grabbed the old man by his shoulders and roughly pulled him towards the water. The old man tumbled into the water with a loud splash. Medusa would hear the old man yelling in anger at first and then panic as the ship continued moving. She turned back and saw him slowly growing smaller as they continued along. In a hurry she turned back to look at the men who were now remaining on the ship.

They seemed initially confused before the man who tossed over the old man said loudly, "This is my ship now."

Medusa was a little surprised how easily this man seemed to take control. The others simply agreed with his proclamation.

One of the men asked, "So what will we do now?"

They glanced towards each other and then turned to look at her. She felt her heart drop when she realized right away that this was not going to be good for her.

The leader of the men asked, "Maybe our passenger has more coin?"

As the others nodded she heard another one state, "Or we could take it out of her in another way."

The others laughed. Glancing from side to side she saw no escape. She did not know how to swim. Off in the distance that they were headed she could see land slowly coming closer. It was most likely the destination that they were headed to. The leader of the men was the first to approach her.

He said in a very lustful tone, "We can check for coins later."

She shuffled backwards to get away from him but he was too quick and was in front of her before she could escape. Pain struck her arm where he grabbed her roughly. She called out in pain.

“She squeals too.” One of the other men stated wickedly.

The other men laughed again. Attempting to move away from the larger man failed as he pulled on her arm yet again.

“Take off that himation so we can get a look at her.” One man stated.

Medusa attempted to fight the man but failed as he pulled on her himation, unwrapping it as he pulled. Her head was fully exposed and the snakes of her hair reacted wildly to their rare moment of freedom. The facial expression of the man holding her arm shifted to panic as he released her.

One of the nearby men screamed out, “It is a monster!”

As she looked at the man who was once holding her arm he already was turning to a stone statue. She started to look around but most of the men on the small ship had started to dive off the side to escape her. Another one looked directly at her as she looked around. He too turned quickly into a stone statue. Medusa could hear the men who had escaped the ship swimming to get away from her. It was not an ideal way to escape but at least she was not in danger. She quickly wrapped her himation back around her head to mask her face. As she stood there trying to decide what to do she realized that the ship she was on was still heading towards land. Panic once again hit her as she realized that the only way she was going to make it to the land in front of her was would be crash into it. She got the idea that it might be wise to hide these statues in case there was someone where she landed.

Pushing as hard as she could on the stone statue of the man who assaulted her she mumbled, “So heavy.”

Heaving as hard as she could she was finally able to overturn the statue, which tumbled into the water and disappeared. She was already out of breath from the effort. The other man who was turned into stone was thankfully standing near the edge of the ship so she was able to nudge him into the water easily. Now she was able to see the land that the ship was headed towards. Off to the right she spotted a village of some kind. She guessed that it was their planned destination of Sami. The ship itself was pointed a good distance away from that village but close enough that Medusa thought she could walk there easily. Not sure what to do with herself she sat down on a bench that was near the front of the ship. As she sat there the wind seemed to continue pushing the ship closer and closer to the land in front of her. As she was able to start to see much better definition of the land in front of her the ship began to turn towards the right and away from where it was headed. Medusa began to panic as she was worried that the ship might end up going out to sea. She stood up and ran to the stick in the back that she had saw the old man playing with and began to push it to try and steer the ship. It was something that she was mostly clueless about. It did not move at all so she shoved even harder to try and move it. Straining as hard as she could she pushed the stick, which finally reacted by moving towards the right. The ship slowly responded by slightly shifting back in the direction that it was originally headed. She continued to hold it in place with all the energy that she had. The ship kept moving along and got closer towards land. After a bit the ship violently slammed into the beach.

CHAPTER 10

Medusa went flying forward and roughly collided the floor of the ship.

"Ooooaaah!" She called out in pain and panic as she caught herself with her hands.

She felt a bruise forming on her left shoulder where she did impact the ship. The ship rocked back for a moment before settling in place on the shore of wherever she now was. Medusa exhaled heavily in relief. It was a miracle that she survived this far. She stood up and glanced around. There was no one in sight and she realized that it was probably not wise to stay there. Moving quickly she searched the ship for anything useful. There was nothing worth taking so she delicately attempted to climb out of the ship where it was sitting on land. As she reached out with her right foot the ship shifted in response and caused her to stumble out onto the beach. She landed on her right side into soft sand. It was a fortunate place to land. Pulling herself off the ground she stood and glanced around. Taking a moment to think she decided to head towards the town that she could see before the ship crashed. The best guess that she could give was that it would take more than a day to get there. Her leftover food was wet from splashing in the water as she fell but otherwise she was good. Dusting off the sand on her chiton she slung her bag on her shoulder and started walking towards the town. She walked for some time and noticed that the sun was beginning to set.

She said to herself, "It is going to be dark before I make it."

Taking a moment to glance around, she found a spot near the edge of the beach that she could sleep for the night. It was along the beach and had a slight incline under some bushes. She pulled out a blanket and laid it down before settling down to get some sleep.

* * * * *

Medusa started awake to the sound of several animals moving nearby. She looked over and saw a herd of goats shuffling along.

As she sat up she heard a male voice say in surprise, "Oh, someone is here."

Making sure her himation was covering her head she turned and looked at the voice. It was a young man, she guessed maybe about her age. He was wearing a simple old dirty chiton and rough looking sandals. In his hand was a long weathered stick.

Standing up she said, "Yes, sorry if I startled you. It was late so I had to sleep."

The boy stiffened up before stating, "I was not startled."

Not wanting to offend him Medusa said, "Of course not, sorry. I was wondering if you could tell me the name of the town down there."

She pointed towards the town that she had seen before the ship she was on crashed.

"Yes. That is Sami." The young man answered.

Giving him a slight nod Medusa said, "Thank you."

Moving in that direction she started to walk. Her best guess was that she would get there about lunch time. She opened her bag and pulled out some dried fruit to eat as she walked. Her guess was a little off as she finally spotted Sami just after noon. The town consisted of about twenty or so various homes made of dried mud bricks, a small number of fancier homes that appeared to be made of stone, and three marble homes. Off to the far right she spotted a big temple. She saw a large statue of Athena, which meant that the temple was for Athena. A deep frown crossed her face. Medusa did not like Athena. Shrugging it off, she headed towards the entrance of the town. After a bit of walking she saw several very normal looking men walking around. They did not seem to notice her at first but once she approached the town they began watching her very closely. She tried to ignore them as she continued along. Eventually she got close to what she thought was the center of the town. It was likely her imagination but she swore that everyone there was staring at her. Suddenly a larger man wearing a heavy leather full length tunic that went down to his knees with a belt wrapped around his waist. A sword was hanging off of it.

He grumpily said, “We do not want homeless girls here.”

She was shocked at his proclamation.

After a moment of stun she finally muttered out, “I am just looking to buy food.”

A woman off to her left yelled out, “Get out of here homeless wretch. We are not feeding beggars.”

“Begone!” A third voice yelled.

Suddenly something struck Medusa on her left shoulder. She turned to look and saw that it was a tomato that hit her. Fear struck her.

The man said firmly as he pointed away from the town and into an open field. “Go.”

Without thinking Medusa began to walk quickly in the direction that he pointed to get away from these people. Something heavier struck her back. It was some kind of vegetable but she did not take the time to look as she started to run away.

“Run away, little beggar!” A different female voice yelled out.

Medusa ran as fast as she could to escape the unusually cruel people. She made it out of the town rapidly and before long she was in the middle of an open field. Trying her best she kept up the pace for a bit longer before she could run no more. She was still in a field but directly in front of her was a large forest that continued on before turning mountainous in the distance. Off to her left she spotted a few farm homes between the wide fields of olive trees, fig trees, and a variety of other fruits. Since there was no one around her, she crept up to a fig tree and helped herself to a few figs before continuing away from Sami. She had no idea where she was headed but anything was better than that town. Their reaction to her extremely confusing. Sure her clothing was a little dirty from when she crashed into the sand and then slept on the ground but she had done nothing to indicate that she was going to beg and yet they treated her so horribly. Giving a mental sigh she continued walking. It was well after noon as the forest came fully into view. Sprinkled along the edge of the forest was the occasional home but overall it was just trees. Medusa began walking into the forest. She came across a small river that headed up towards the mountainous area. Kneeling down she used her hand to cup some water to drink. She was quite thirsty and the cool water tasted wonderful. The forest smelled pleasant enough and she could hear the sound of birds chirping and a variety of insects clicking. Following the path of the river she continued along. Something was guiding her towards the mountains so she kept walking. As she kept moving along she spotted something unusual off to her right. It looked like a home except it had no roof. Because of the tree cover she was struggling to see very well so she removed her himation to help her see a little easier. Stepping closer she realized that it was an old beat up home that had the roof caved in by a large branch. Searching through the home she found dirty chairs, a small table, and some very grimy looking clay dishes. She thought to stay in the home but it was completely ruined. Turning back to the small river she once again headed towards the towering mountains. Finally, after walking for a bit more the small river that she was following ended into a pretty looking pond. The pond was wedged up against a tall mountainside cliff that had water running down it and into the pond. She stopped once again to drink more water before looking to her left or right. Suddenly she felt a drop of rain splash down on her head. She had been wearing the himation for so long, virtually all the time, that she forgot how nice it was not to wear it. Another drop hit her. Glancing up she realized that it was about to rain quite heavily.

"Dang it." She muttered to herself.

Looking to her left and then right she thought that she spotted what looked like a cave off to her right. It was not ideal but she just needed to get out of the rain that was starting to come down in earnest. Jogging over to the cave she peeked in real fast. It was about the side of a large bedroom and appeared dry. As she stepped in she sighed. It was relief to get out of the soaking rain. Her chiton was already drenched. Flipping off her bag, which was soaked as well, she dug through it to get her blankets out. Even the blankets were wet. Sighing heavily she spread out one of them on the ground to at least have something to sit on. Glancing out the entrance of the cave she watched the rain poor heavily down. It was then that it dawned on her what had happened. She was now a hideous monster living in a cave on a secluded island. That realization caused her to feel utter despair and before long she found herself crying. Flinging herself onto the ground on her blanket she sobbed uncontrollably.

FIVE YEARS LATER

CHAPTER 11

Medusa rolled off of her crudely made cloth bed as the sound of her rooster crowing loudly echoed into her ears. Sunlight had begun to peek through her cave. She stood up and glanced back at her bed. It was made of scraps of cloth that she pilfered from the dilapidated home that she had found along the river. She had initially stuffed it with leaves but as she explored the area around the forest she found a large sheep farm near a very small village by the edge of the forest that she was in. She had sneakily sheered enough wool from them to fill her bed, which made it amazingly comfortable to sleep on. Part of all the training that her mother gave her in preparation to be a wife was learning how to make and maintain clothing. She made herself several new chiton out of wool and a few pairs of sandals. Her rooster crowed loudly again.

"I am coming, I am coming." Medusa called out.

She stretched her arms upwards. The snakes on her head hissed and flailed about as she stretched. Something in her head imagined that they reacted to what she did and usually emulated her. It was probably just her own imagination running wild but honestly what else did she have to do? Slipping on her chiton and sandals she stepped outside of her cave. She had dug out a small garden along the entrance of the cave and the cliff-side towards the pond. It was easily big enough to grow enough fruit and vegetables for her to eat throughout the year. It took her some time to make the garden but it was worth it since now she would not have to spend her time raiding people's homes for food.

Eventually they would find out and turn on her. She picked up a handful of grain and sprinkled it on the ground.

"Eat up." She told her chicken.

Medusa had borrowed the rooster and about ten chicken from several of the farms just outside the forest. Stealing was her primary source of setting up her own private little farm. She stole the seeds for her garden, the chicken she kept was for eggs, the occasional fish for meat, and a few pieces of furniture for her cave. After feeding her chicken she started to tend her small garden. She bounced from the tomatoes, the onions, the cabbage, and the peppers as she plucked out a few weeds that had sprouted up. Over the first year of her garden she built a small wicker fence around it to keep out small animals like frogs. Checking the nests of her chicken she found a few eggs. It would make for a nice meal. She found that frying the eggs with pieces of vegetables in them tasted very nice. After making herself a quick breakfast she cleaned up her mess. Something had told her that it was wise to keep her use of fire limited so she usually only lit it for making food. At night she would use several woolen blankets to keep warm on the rare times it got too cold at night.

As she finished cleaning she decided to bathe so she turned to her chicken and announced, "Georgios keep an eye on the ladies while I am gone."

The rooster clucked at her before he pecked again at some of the grain that Medusa had sprinkled on the ground for him. Giving a light chuckle she grabbed one of her blankets and a fresh change of clothing. She had turned the nearby pond into her own private bath tub and while the water was cold usually, she was happy to bathe regularly. After a short walk she was at the pond. The water felt cool and she was enjoyed her bath. The last four years had been very lonely but it was pleasant not to be chased by anyone. As she dipped her head into the pond she decided she would sneak over to the nearest village to see if she could find a bucket. It would be nice to store her chicken's grain in. As she dried off with one of her blankets she heard one of her chicken clucking nearby. It was one of the hens. She recognized it immediately.

With a giggle Medusa asked, “Anthousa, why do you keep sneaking out of the fence?”

That one hen was always sneaking out. Medusa worried for her because it was not safe in the forest. She had seen several wild animals who would gobble poor Anthousa up if given a chance. One of the earliest things that she discovered while living on Kefalonia was that animals seemed completely unaffected by her curse. She first realized it when she was sneaking around stealing wool. One of the sheep had looked directly at her face and nothing happened. She purposely tried to see if a wide variety of other animals would be turned to stone by her gaze but none seemed to. In fact most animals seemed to react in an unusually calm manner towards her. Wild animals that would run from most seemed to just ignore her as though she was one of them.

Slipping on her chiton and sandals she gestured Anthousa towards the pen as she stated, “Come on silly girl.”

Once Medusa had her hen back into the fenced pen she closed it shut and then grabbed her himation. The only time she wore it was when she was away from her small cave. If she ran into someone she would not accidentally turn them into stone statue. For some reason she suspected if people found out she was here it would be a cause of serious issues for her. She just wanted to be left alone. Slowly she headed off towards the small village. It consisted of only a small handful of homes and a group of booths that served as a trading market. She still had quite a few coins from the men who attacked her in Athens. If she could steal what she needed she would avoid spending them. Most of what she had spent was early on when she first settled down in the cave. Once she got her garden working she did not need to buy much of anything. Her best guess was it was over three years ago. Living alone she lost track of time, in fact she was not even sure what time of year it was. She had a vague idea based on the season but honestly all that did not matter to her. The weather was quite pleasant as she strolled along in the forest. It was a short walk to the outskirts of the village. She skulked along from tree to tree and behind a few bushes as she scouted around looking for a bucket. There was not one within sight. She realized that her best option would be to just cave in and see if one was for sale at the booths. Making sure to firmly pull her himation around her she walked into the village.

As she approached one of the booths an older woman in a dingy white chiton said, "Good morning young lady."

Making sure to keep looking down Medusa softly replied, "Good morning."

"Do you need anything?"

"I was wondering if you knew if someone had a bucket for sale."

The woman paused for a moment before saying, "Oh yes, I believe that Zosimus sells all sorts of things and probably would have one for sale."

The woman pointed over towards a man who Medusa guessed was in his mid-thirties. Honestly throughout her whole time in Athens she found that she was horrible at guessing ages.

Giving a light nod Medusa said to the woman, "Thank you."

"Of course."

Turning around Medusa approached the man. He was in the middle of a discussion with another man about something going on in their village. It had to do with some sort of politics and people in Sami. It appeared that the leadership of Sami were increasing taxes on every person on the island and people in the village were not happy about it. If she had to worry about such things Medusa felt that she probably would have been upset as well. During the many conversations of her father's that she spied on she heard that taxes was the primary way that governments could fund themselves. Her father railed against Athenian taxes constantly.

Her train of thought was interrupted when the man at the booth asked, "Young lady may I help you with something?"

Startled out of her own thoughts Medusa answered, "Yes, I was told that you might have a bucket that I could purchase."

The main nodded at her before responding, "Stay right here. I have a wood bucket back in my home I can sell you."

"Alright."

The man turned and left for a moment. Medusa remained quiet as the other man who was talking with the owner of the booth stood there awkwardly. She was not comfortable trying to talk with him so she said nothing. After a long uncomfortable pause the man returned with a simple looking wooden bucket.

"I can sell it to you for one drachma."

The price seemed a bit high to Medusa but she had little need for coins so she just nodded before digging out one silver drachma. She passed it over to the man who then handed her the bucket.

"Thank you." She told him.

Tucking the coin into a pouch the man told her, "Of course."

She hefted the wooden bucket and as she walked away examined it. Within the bucket was a thick coating of a waxy substance. Her best guess was it was designed to keep water in. She headed down the pathway away from the village and once she was completely out of sight of the village she turned back around. Her time away from her home back in Piraeus taught her to be very paranoid. Constant fear that she was about to be attacked was something that filled her with dread whenever she was near people. It was quite pleasing to see that no one was following her. She headed off the pathway for the village and towards the forest where her home was. After she got deep enough into the forest that she knew no one would find her, she slipped off her himation. The snakes on her head flailed a brief moment before settling down. She found herself wishing she could control them at least but that did not seem to be something she could do no matter how hard she tried. It was obvious that they did react to her mood however. When she was mad or angry they got agitated. If she was happy they seemed calm. Once she had settled into her cave she had thought on it and tried her hardest to control them. At this point in her life she gave up on worrying about them and just did what she needed to in order to survive. She made it to the small stream and as she strolled along she spotted the beat up home that she had pilfered for a few things. Her best guess was that she had dug through that place like ten or so times. There was some movement coming from the building. Medusa's heart dropped, someone must have followed her and she did not see them. Moving as fast as she could, she wrapped her himation around her head to cover her hideous face. Cautiously she approached the home. Her stomach roiled with nervousness. She really did not want to turn some villager into a stone statue. Right as she hit the corner she heard the sound of a chicken clucking. Pecking on the ground near the entrance of the home was a chicken, specifically it was one of hers.

"Anthousa! How in the world did you get out here?"

Medusa was extremely relieved.

As she slowly picked up the hen she stated, "It is not safe for you out here."

The hen clucked in response. Medusa was confident that this silly chicken was going to get herself killed. She tucked it under her arm and started walking. It was a brief walk before she made it back to her cave. After opening the pen for her chicken she set Anthousa down and then closed the pen.

Gesturing with her right index finger Medusa stated huffily, "Young lady stay in this pen."

Shifting away she grinned to herself. That hen had been slipping out constantly for some reason. Moving over to her grain that she had been feeding the chicken, she lifted the rough bag that it was in and dumped the grain into her new bucket. It held nicely and it will allow her to move around easier to feed her chicken. Setting down the bucket she turned around examine her small little home. It was not a huge marble home like she was supposed to have moved into after being married but it was hers and it had everything that she needed. Letting out a deep sigh she went into her cave and picked up the sword that she had taken from the men who attacked her in Athens. Since she settled down in Kefalonia she used the sword to hunt the forest for wild mushrooms. She had found the mushrooms that grew in the forest to be tasty with eggs and fried. It also was a nice variation on her normal diet. One of the good things about her lifestyle was that the excessive walking around the forest had gotten her into quite good shape. It also helped her learn every little bit of the forest. Snatching up her other himation, which she flung over her shoulder, she headed off. From her many other wanderings in the forest she had a great idea where all the best spots for mushrooms were at. Of course she was proven right when she got to the first spot that she guessed some real nice ones would be.

“Oooo!” She exclaimed when she got to her first spot.

There was easily thirty or so mushrooms growing up against an old tree but in a shady spot. She examined several of the mushrooms carefully to make sure she did not accidentally pick a toxic one. During her first few weeks of living on the island she had eaten a bad mushroom before and was sick for days because of it. Once she recovered she went to the small village and examined the mushrooms they were eating, she even bought a few, to make sure she would not get one that made her sick again. At this point she was an expert on mushrooms. Tenderly setting down her himation she cut several mushrooms and placed them on it. She generally only picked enough for a few days since they would go bad quickly. Once she had enough she folded her himation in half and then picked it up. Casually strolling along she admired the weather. During the winter she found it rained a lot, especially compared to Athens. It also got quite muggy as well. She guessed that it was late fall and it was lovely. Deciding that she had enough mushrooms for now she headed back to her cave. After setting down her mushrooms she picked up the lyre that she had found in the old home. It was pretty dirty from sitting outside in the house but once she cleaned it up she discovered that it was in good condition. Over the last four years, since she found it, she tried to teach herself how to play it. Pretty much every day she would spend time attempting to play the lyre. Back in Piraeus her oldest sister, Stethno, learned how to play it and got very good at it. Medusa had no one to teach her so she just had to plug along on her own. She thought that she was decent at playing it but with nothing else to do with her free time she kept at it, hoping to get better.

The first pluck of a string was horribly off-key so she mumbled, “Ewww.”

She tuned it a little before playing around with it for a while. It was starting to get late in the day so she put away her lyre and prepared dinner. She washed some mushrooms, a few other vegetables, and bits of fresh fish that she had got yesterday before making it into a soup. She ate and cleaned up her mess before deciding to sleep. Tomorrow she planned to sneak out and get more fish so she wanted to be well rested. Lying down on her bed she closed her eyes. She drifted off to sleep quickly.

CHAPTER 12

Medusa woke the next morning to the sound of Georgios' loud squawking. She stretched as she stood up. The only good thing about having her own place was the bed she made. It was extremely comfortable because of all of the light fresh wool she packed into it. Also she made it huge, easily big enough for three people. She figured if she was going to be stuck there she might as well be comfortable. After feeding her chicken and playing with her garden she ate breakfast. Next she grabbed some clean clothing before heading off to the pond. After taking a quick bath she wrapped her himation around her head once again before grabbing her bag that she got from the men who attacked her in Athens. She had not returned to Sami since she first arrived but there was a small village north of Sami that she found was a perfect place to get some fresh fish. She tried not to steal when possible and the people there just left her alone with a net. It took her some time to catch a few fish but generally she left with a four or five fish.

Pointing back towards her pen she called out, "Anthousa, you better not sneak out!"

Chuckling to herself she started to walk. It was going to take most of her morning to make it to the village, even at her brisk pace. One great thing about all of the walking she has done over the last few years was that it had turned her body into that of a lean, fit, and pretty muscular grown woman. Every day she probably walked or ran several dozen stadion. The weather was a bit cloudy but very pleasant. It took her about half the morning to make it to the outskirts of the village that she was headed towards. Just like the last few times that she had been there, no one seemed to notice or care about her. Medusa did not know why but the people in this town had a large group of nets that they just left on racks standing near the docks. Anyone could use them and she had used them several times since she settled in. It took her several tries before she finally was able to catch a fish. Her technique was to walk out into the water up to her waist and then tossed the net out as far as she could before dragging it in. Each time she caught a fish she put it into the bag that she had slung over her shoulder. Finally right around lunch time she felt that she had caught enough fish to last her a few days so she walked back to shore to replace the fishing net on the rack that she got it from.

Medusa was quite surprised when an older woman waved at her and said, "Have a good day young lady."

Keeping her head down Medusa replied, "Thank you."

Taking firm steps she walked away from the village towards the main pathway before turning off towards the forest. As usual she glanced back behind her to make sure no one was following her. There were people milling about at the edge of the small village but none of them seemed to notice her slipping off of the path and into the wilds. It was her usual shortcut to the forest. The spot of farmland that she was walking through was an orchard that was growing olives. Trying not to be obvious about picking olives she casually plucked a few from this branch or that branch as she went. She would then tuck several handfuls into her bag while continuing. It was her usual method to get a few olives without staying still. After all, the last thing she wanted to do was draw attention to herself. Back in Piraeus she used to cleanse herself in a mixture of pumice and olive oil but out in the wild it seemed like a waste of time. Now she just used the olives to make oil for cooking or to eat them. The forest where she lived came into view.

Suddenly a male voice off to her right asked, "Did you bring enough bags?"

Shocked at hearing someone speak near the forest she stopped in her tracks.

Another male voice responded, “Yes. Stop worrying Erastus. This village will never know what hit it and we will be off with everything of value.”

She heard another person laugh at the man’s comment. Ducking down she tried to hide behind one of the nearby olive trees. Panic struck her. The last thing that she needed in her life was a group of men harassing her. The sound of the footsteps of the men got louder as they came closer to her. She peeked out and could now see them. It was a group of about seven younger men. They all appeared to be soldiers as each was wearing a leather tunic and had a belted sheath with a sword on it. Walking in the front of the group was a bold looking man that she guessed was in her mid-twenties. He had unmanaged black hair and a scruffy beard that she guessed he had been growing for some time. Just how he carried himself let her know that he was in charge, especially since the other men followed closely behind him. She ducked her head back when she thought that one of them looked in her direction.

One of the men whispered barely loud enough for her to hear, “I think there is someone over there.”

They spotted her! She quickly glanced from side to side. Behind her was an open orchard of olive trees and in front of her was her forest. She guessed her only hope was to make it into the forest and try to lose them there. The idea to turn them into stone hit her but she realized that doing so here in the orchard would let people living nearby know that something unusual was going on. It would put her at extreme risk if the stories about her from Athens had made their way here. She calculated that her best bet was to make a break for the forest and if they caught her then she would deal with them there. At least the stone statues would be hidden in a forest that she knew very few people ever went into. Swallowing down fear, she clenched her hands and then ran as fast as she could towards the forest.

“There she is!” One of them exclaimed.

"Catch her! If she heard our plans it could ruin everything." The man who she guessed was the leader commanded loudly.

Medusa ran as fast as she could with her heart beating hard. The sound of the men who started running after her echoed in her ears. She realized even with her increased fitness that she probably could not outrun a group of healthy soldiers. At this point of running she decided that her best bet was to get as far as she could before turning on them and removing her himation. This was going to be her first time purposefully attempting to use her curse to her advantage. Thankfully for her, the sun was out well enough that even in the forest it was easy to see. These men would not be able to avoid her curse once she turned on them. She swerved hard to her left when she could hear one of the men was very close to her.

"Damn, she is quick!" The man exclaimed as she slipped out of his grasp.

Finally she realized that her run was about to come to an end so she tried to find a small open area. Turning quickly, she stopped around and spun to face the men. They all stopped running only a few arm's lengths away from her.

The man who she guessed was the leader asked, "What did you hear girl?"

Medusa said nothing to them as she took one step backwards.

Another of the men stated angrily, "She heard it all."

This time a different man spoke, "What are we going to do with her Nicephorus?"

"Well," The man who was their leader answered, "We will have to deal with her permanently. She was kind enough to find a nice quiet place for us too."

The first man who asked the question then interjected, "We could have fun with her too. She is looking quite fit."

The other men chuckled at him. Medusa was sickened by them. They were clearly bandits and quite evil. All of the nervousness of the situation completely passed over her and now she was angry.

Squaring her shoulders she announced, "The lot of you have greater concerns than how fit I am."

“Oh yes?” Nicephorus responded.

“Yes,” Medusa declared as she slowly removed her himation before continuing, “You ran into a monster not a girl.”

As she removed her himation the reaction of fear and panic immediately crossed the brows of all seven men. One of them was able to manage a slight scream before his voice gargled silent. She scanned at each man and watched as they all slowly turned into stone statues. It was the first time that she was happy to have been cursed by the cruel goddess Athena. Slapping her himation over her shoulder Medusa walked up to the leader and grabbed his coin purse.

As she opened it and peeked in she commented, “Well at least you were kind enough to help me.”

There was several drachma. Based on her current lifestyle the coins would last her quite a while. After pilfering the coins from the other men she started walking back home. The spot in the forest that the men now stood was far enough away from her cave that she felt confident that no one would know where she was. Of course that was assuming anyone even stumbled across them. It was deep in the forest. As she started to walk home she realized that she might have accidentally helped the village that she regularly visited. The men were headed in that direction and were talking about robbing them. She suspected that they might have even killed someone in order to get their way. Just on accident she probably saved someone’s life. It made her feel a little better. The panic of the moment had long since passed and now she was reflecting about it all. Medusa continued on her way. She needed to get home quickly to clean these fish because they would go bad real fast if she did not. The plan was to skin, gut, and cut them into manageable pieces. She was going to cook some of it for supper tonight and the rest she would have to dry out for the next couple days. Once she finished that she would need to crush the olives to get the oil out of them. It was all going to keep her quite busy for the next two days. Her distraction was interrupted by the sound of movement in the brushes. She initially panicked but then a brown flash of fur caught her eye. It was one of those dang hare. During one of her visits to the village she heard that they tasted very good in stew and she has tried many times to catch one with a sharpened stick. It had been one of her biggest failures. She decided tomorrow to put off pressing olives and try to catch one again, maybe she would finally succeed. As she approached the cave she saw that her pen was once again nudged open.

She called out loudly, “Anthousa!”

A clucking sound came from off to her right. Glancing over she spotted a hen that she immediately recognized as Anthousa. That hen was trouble from the moment Medusa swiped her. Setting down her bag Medusa picked up Anthousa and put her back in the pen before closing the gate. Medusa had no clue how she kept getting out. It was secure enough that none of the other chicken, even Georgios, would escape but yet Anthousa kept finding a way to open it. While she did not want to admit it, Medusa was glad she took Anthousa. That silly hen probably brought the only joy that she had in her life. She just hoped nothing bad happened to the bird when Medusa was out and about. Picking up her bag she slowly removed all of the olives and placed them into a large wooden bowl. They would sit fine for a few days but the fish needed to be dealt with immediately. She laid out a stained woolen cloth and set each of the fish down before taking a knife out and slowly gutting each one. It was smelly and dirty work but once she finished she was quite pleased. The excess parts of the fish would draw small animals like fox and a variety of lizards so she walked a good distance to dispose of them. She returned and cut the fish into nice pieces before frying some of it up to eat. The rest she set out on a high rock to dry. Next she placed a wicker basket over the fish. It was a hard lesson that she learned when early on she had set fish out and a pack of birds stole all of it.

Turning back around she spotted Anthousa sneaking over towards the gate of the pen so she called out, “Do not do it silly bird.”

Anthousa strutted back over to the middle of the pen. Medusa chuckled. It was close to supper time so she picked a few vegetables to cook. Mixing the vegetables with water and chunks of fish she made herself some stew. She really wanted bread to go with it but there was no way to bake it without a stove. The stew still tasted good and after she cleaned up she felt much better. It was late enough in the day that she decided to postpone hunting those pesky hare until tomorrow morning. Instead she started to press the olives. Back when she was collecting items for her cave she was able to find one large jar. She now used it to keep olive oil in. Taking up her mortar and pestle, some of the few items she did have to buy, she slowly pressed each olive individually. It was a very slow and tedious process however she had plenty of time and not much else to do so she kept at it. It also did not hurt that olive oil made everything taste better when used to cook as a motivating factor to perform the tedious task. The sun began to set so Medusa decided that she should clean up and get some sleep. She strolled over to the pond and dipped her hands in to wash them. After she felt cleaner she went back to her cave. It felt like it was going to be a bit colder night so she made sure to get one of her extra wool blankets to sleep with. Almost the moment she laid down she found herself drifting off to sleep.

CHAPTER 13

Once again the sound of Georgios squawking loudly woke Medusa. She stood up and stretched. She chuckled when Anthousa came strutting into the cave. That hen really just did whatever she wanted to. Right before checking her garden Medusa fed her chicken and then headed off for a bath. Today she was going to try once again to catch a hare. After bathing she got dressed and grabbed her sharpened stick. She used the sword that she got in Athens to sharpen it. Honestly it was one of the few things that she had in her possession that not been useful since she moved to Kefalonia. Maybe today was the day that it would finally prove useful? She had to rinse out her bag because it smelled like fish and once it was clean she brought it back to her cave. Taking some fruit from her garden and a few pieces of dried fish she packed them into her bag. Once she felt ready, she started to head off.

Taking a second to turn back she pointed at Anthousa with her stick and declared firmly, "Stay there you bad girl."

The hen scratched her foot onto the ground before giving off a slight clucking noise. Medusa continued walking. The best places that she saw hare at was generally closer to the outskirts of the forest by the farms. She guessed that it might have been because of the more easily available food for the hare but allowed for a quick escape back into the forest. Today the weather was slightly cloudy with a subtle breeze that gently pushed into her face. It felt nice and the woody smell of the forest only made the walk more enjoyable. She had to admit that she found the fresh air of Kefalonia much better than Athens, which tended to have had a foul smell of too many people. As she approached the edge of the forest she wrapped a himation around her head. After all, she had no plans to turn some random farmer into a stone statue. She just wanted to catch a hare for dinner. Being careful to look around before entering the farm she spotted no one. This part of the farm looked like rows of small plants. They were wide-leafed cucumber plants. Some smaller undeveloped cucumbers were laying on the ground. Kneeling down she examined one. A leaf from it was gnawed upon and one of the small cucumbers appeared someone or something ate part of it. This was surely something done by a hare. Sitting perfectly still she listened. For some time it was quiet but eventually she heard something rustling in the nearby bushes.

Whispering as quietly as she could Medusa said, “Got you.”

Attempting to move sneak along as much as she could Medusa took a step towards the sound. She watched where she was stepping to make sure that she did not step on anything that would make noise. Carefully, step by step, she moved closer to the sound. Finally she was able to see what was making the noise. It was a light brown hare with long ears and a white fluffy tail. She had never seen one this close before. Honestly she had to admit that it was a cute animal but she heard they tasted delicious in a stew and she was growing tired of fish. She hefted her stick with the sharp end facing towards the hare. Pulling the stick backwards she took aim before throwing it as hard as she could at the creature. The stick went flying and missed the hare by a good distance before clattering against the ground. The hare ran as fast as it could into the nearby forest.

“Dang!” She exclaimed loudly.

Medusa was utterly disappointed that she missed the creature. It was going to be hard to find more of them. Strolling over to her stick she picked it up. A firm wave of determination hit her. She decided that she was not going to quit so easily. Hefting her stick once again she slowly crept along and stopped several times to listen. It took her almost until lunch time to find another hare. She lined herself as best as she could and fired off her stick at it. Sadly she missed again, although she was much closer this time than the last. After picking up her stick she walked back into the forest a bit before sitting down and eating lunch from her bag. She was quite hungry from all the sneaking about and crouching so she gobbled her lunch very quickly. Once she was done she slipped her bag over her shoulder and again hefted her stick. Cautiously walking back to the edges of the forest she decided to work her way further from the nearest village. She guessed that maybe there would be more hare farther away from other people. It was a little bit of a walk but she finally got far enough that she felt was in a good spot. Slowly kneeling down she stopped to listen carefully. After a few moments she heard something rustling nearby. It was much louder than anything she heard before and piqued her curiosity. Stealthily she moved closer to the sound and after a few moments she was surprised to realize that what was making the noise was a hideous loud creature that was rubbing its back into the small tree surrounded by shrubs. It stood slightly up past her knees and walked on four legs with a wide barrel body, two disk-shaped hairy ears, a heavy coat of stringy fur that dangled off its body, and a longer narrow snout with two tusks coming out of its mouth. It was grunting and snuffling as it rubbed itself against the tree through the bushes. Medusa realized immediately that she did not want to tangle with whatever it was so she began to creep away. As she stepped backwards she accidentally stepped onto a small branch. It made a loud cracking noise as it broke in half. She stopped immediately to try and not make any more noise. The creature stopped rubbing itself against the tree and made an unusual noise.

"Oh no." Medusa said softly as the creature moved away from the tree and headed towards her.

Panicking since she knew that her curse did not affect animals she dashed as fast as she could away from the creature. It made a loud noise and began to chase her. She did not mean to but she accidentally dropped her stick while trying to run as fast as she could back into the forest. The creature was still running behind her and based on how much noise it was making she knew that it was gaining on her. It dawned on her that she needed to find some way to escape it by going somewhere that it could not follow her. She peeked back at the creature to confirm that it was gaining on her. One thing of note she realized was that it had hooved feet. Maybe her best bet would be to climb into a tree out of its reach. Off ahead of her she found a tree with a low enough branch that she could get a hold of and climb onto. Jumping upwards she grabbed the branch with both hands and used her feet to try and push onto the trunk of the tree. It allowed her the ability to pull herself onto the tree. Moving a bit closer towards the trunk Medusa fully got onto the branch and tucked her body into a ball balanced on the branch. The creature ran into the tree causing it to vibrate slightly but the tree was stable enough that she knew it would not be knocked down by it. The beast grunted and groaned as it paced nearby. It was obviously agitated by Medusa interrupting it back in the farm.

Letting out a heavy sigh Medusa whispered, "Why me?"

Every time she felt comfortable it always seemed as though something bad happened to her. She had no idea how long this dumb beast would hover around waiting to attack her. Without her stick she would have no way to fend it off, especially if it did manage to get a hold of her. She sat up on that branch for what felt like an eternity before the sun began to set. Finally the creature gave up and shuffled off back towards the field that it was in when she ran into it. Something told her to wait for a bit before climbing down. While she was sure that the creature was not overly intelligent she did not know if it would come back if it heard her. Once she was confident that the beast was gone she delicately climbed down. There was no way she was going to find her stick in the dark so she just headed back home to her cave. The noise from a variety of small animals and insects echoed in her ears as she trudged back to her cave. She was quite happy to see it but her joy was immediately crushed when she realized that her pen was open and Anthousa was once again missing.

"Anthousa!" She called out desperately.

The sounds of her other chicken scratching and clucking were the only response to her sad call for her favorite hen. She walked around a bit looking in all of the places that she had seen Anthousa wandering before. There was nothing. It was becoming so dark that she could not see anymore. Sadness struck her as she realized that she was not going to find her chicken in the dark. Begrudgingly she headed back to her cave. As she hung her bag over the fencing of her pen she stomped into her cave. She removed her sandals before sadly flopping onto her bed. Worrying thoughts about Anthousa caused her to struggle falling asleep but she finally was able to drift off late into the night.

* * * * *

Georgios' squawking early in the morning startled Medusa out of sleep. She sat up immediately and remembered that Anthousa was missing. In a hurry she stood up and put on her sandals. Stepping out of her cave she was surprised to see Anthousa standing right next to the pen! All of Medusa's panic was for nothing. That dang hen came back, which Medusa knew was just because of the easy and free food.

Letting out a heavy sigh of relief Medusa stated in a chiding tone, "Young lady you cannot keep doing this to me. I almost died last night when I came back to you missing!"

Anthousa simply looked up at Medusa before tilting her head sideways. Giving a shrug Medusa picked up her bucket of grain as she started feeding all of her chicken. She decided that she needed to find something to secure her pen better because she could not be worrying about Anthousa or the others while she was out and about during the day. The only thing that she could think of that would work would be to replace the long sticks that she drove into the ground with actual posts. It dawned on her that the best place to go was the village and just buy them. Maybe Anthousa was wedging through the cloth swathes that made up the pen between the branches. She figured that she should replace them with weave used for baskets that was made of thin wood. It might take her a few days to collect and make it all but it would be worth it to protect her chicken. She decided to skip a bath until she got back with her supplies. Making sure to grab her bag, himation, and coin purse she headed off to the village. Her walk to the village took about as long as normal and she made sure to wrap her himation around her head. As every other time she entered the village, no one said a word to her. She was thankful for it because it seemed as though they just accepted her as someone who must have lived in an outlying farm. She went to the booths and approached the man who she bought a bucket from. This time he was standing all by himself.

"You have returned." The man stated before asking, "How is that bucket working for you?"

Keeping her head down Medusa answered, "Well, thank you."

"Well I am guessing you want to buy something else." He stated after a moment.

"Yes." She answered.

"And what do you need now?"

"I am building a chicken pen so I need strong posts and several weave baskets."

The man paused thoughtfully for a moment before he stated, "I can sell you baskets but you will need to talk to Hilarion in order to get the posts."

"Hilarion?"

The man pointed down the pathway before answering, "Yes he sells wood. Speak to him and he should be able to help. Now… how many baskets do you think you will need?"

Pausing for a moment to ponder the question she answered, "About ten."

"Alright, give me a moment. I will need another drachma for that many."

"Okay." She responded.

The man walked away and started talking to several others with a booth. After a bit of a longer wait than she expected he finally returned with two handful of baskets. She paid him and took the baskets. They were heavy enough and took both of her hands to carry so she decided that she would have to take them home before going back for the wood posts.

Turning back to the man she said, "Thank you."

"You are welcome young lady."

She trudged down the pathway and made sure no one was following her before turning off towards the forest. It was a bit slower going since she had to awkwardly carry the baskets but eventually she made it to the edge of the forest. Out of paranoia she glanced back once again to see if anyone was behind her. It was pleasant that she made it this far without being followed by either another person or that big ugly beast. Turning forward she began to walk through the forest. It was getting just a bit past lunch time so she was ready to eat. As she walked along she suddenly heard someone or something trudging clumsily through the forest. She mumbled to herself in fear. It was probably that dang beast from earlier. Stopping to see what it was she caught sight of not an ugly beast but a man! He was clumsily stumbling through the forest with his hands flailing out as though he was walking in the dark. It was quite confusing to her. He was wearing a bedraggled and heavily stained leather tunic that covered a chiton, a pair of sandals, and around his waist was a belt. He looked like a soldier but he had no weapon on him. Like every man she had seen he had heavily tanned skin, black hair, and a beard. The only thing of note about him was he seemed to have what looked like burn marks across his face by his eyes and bridge of his nose.

The man's voice called out in what she guessed was a nervous tone, "Hello? I know I heard someone out there."

She stayed purposely quiet in the hope he would give up and stumble on his way.

The man then said, "Please help me. I am blind and lost."

CHAPTER 14

Medusa's heart dropped. If this man was not lying then he was in serious danger wandering the woods alone and blind. She tried to harden her heart to turn away but her mother had always talked about charity and helping those in need. Could she ignore lessons taught her whole life for her own selfish purpose? Slowly she tried to step away but something stopped her. It just was not right.

Deciding to at least help the man to the village she stepped forward and said, "Hold on."

The man's head shifted in her general direction before he almost joyfully responded, "Thank you so much. I got lost from my group and have been wandering for a long time."

Stepping closer to the man she saw why he was flailing his arms as though he could not see. His eyes appeared murky looking. It was then that she realized he was blind, just as he had claimed. Once she got closer the man gave her a smile. She could see that he was both quite fit and an attractive man with a firm jawline. His beard was full but neatly trimmed. Her best guess was that he was around twenty five years old.

As she moved just outside his reach he asked, "Could you help me find water? I have not drank in what I think are a few days."

"Of course." She told him before continuing, "Follow me."

He laughed at her before stating, "I am going to need help. I cannot see where you are."

Medusa hesitated because she was not so sure that she wanted to get within arm's reach of a stranger, even if he was blind. She realized that if he really was blind there would be no way that he could follow her. Deciding to test if he really was blind she waved her hand in front of him. He did not respond. The ultimate test came to her mind as she stood there. Slowly she unwrapped her himation and once she had her head fully exposed she looked right into his eyes. Nothing happened. He was standing there looking off into the distance. Sighing she shifted her baskets to one arm before reaching out her left arm out and brushing it against his outstretched right hand. He grasped her forearm firmly but not so tight as to hurt her.

"Thank you. Could we get some water?" He asked.

"Sure." She told him before slowly turning to guide him to the nearby small river.

They walked along slowly. Medusa was curious about how he got into the forest and what happened to his eyes. She was not sure it was a polite question to ask. Most likely she would be better off just helping him get water and then get him to the village.

As they walked the man asked, "Are we in grove or forest?"

Quietly she answered, "A forest."

"It is hard to tell except I can feel the shade and I kept bumping into trees." The man stated with a light chuckle.

Medusa chuckled at his obvious joke.

After a bit more walking the man asked her, "What is your name?"

"Medusa." She answered.

"I am Proetus of Argos."

Medusa did not respond. She had never met someone from Argos but she had heard of it. Her father had talked with many of his friends about the other cities that traded with Athens and Argos was one of those cities. That was all she knew about it. They finally reached the small river.

"We are here." She told him,

"I can hear it. Is it a creek?"

"A small river."

"Guide me please." He asked.

She took his hand and then gently guided him down to the river. He knelt as she moved downward and once his hand hit the water he greedily used his hands to scoop water and drink it. Medusa stood nearby patiently waiting while he continued drinking for some time.

Finally he stood up and said, "Thank you. I do not suppose you can help me get something to eat? I am quite hungry."

She frowned. The last thing that she wanted to do was give him food.

"I was going to take you to a village just outside of the forest."

"What is it called?" Proetus asked.

Taking a moment to try and remember the name of the village she finally got it, "Poulata."

"Ahh. How far is it from here?"

"Half a day or so walk."

"Could I eat something first? It has been a while since I last ate."

Giving out a slight sigh Medusa caved in as she answered, "Alright."

Proetus must have sensed her hesitance because he quickly stated, "You need not worry for I am harmless."

Medusa grunted softly. She had grown to distrust men completely because of everything that had happened to her. Since he was blind she felt much safer in dealing with him. She decided to take him to the cave and give him something to eat. At least she had a sword so if he tried anything she could just deal with him herself.

"Alright, let us go get you some food. I have a few things in my cave."

"Cave?" Proetus asked curiously.

She flushed. It was not intentional on her part to let him know that she lived in a cave but since it was already out she decided to just admit it.

"Yes. It is very nice." She stated resolutely.

She was not about to be shamed by some blind man. Maybe she should just take him to the village instead.

"That is good. I just greatly appreciate the help. I would have died if not for you." He stated sincerely.

"You are welcome. Shall we head off?" She asked while very relieved that he made no comment about her home.

He reached his right hand out, which she set her left arm under for him to grasp. Once he got a hold of her arm she began to walk him towards her cave. She found herself unusually nervous as they walked along. It was getting close to supper time so she was not surprised that he did not want to wait to eat, especially if he had not eaten anything in over a day. Her cave came into view and the first thing that she noticed was the fact that Anthousa was still in the pen. Medusa could only guess that whatever happened the night before had kept her in the pen.

She guided Proetus to one of her chairs that was sitting next the opening of her cave and had him sit before saying, "Let me make something for dinner."

"Alright, thank you."

Giving him a nod, she turned to set down the armful of baskets. Her arm was more than a little sore from holding them all in one arm. Moving into the pen that she held her chicken she collected all of the eggs that she could. It would take plenty of them to feed a probably very hungry man. She set the eggs into one of the baskets and then used another to collect some vegetables from her garden. Starting a small fire, she cracked each egg one by one pouring the egg into the pot. Next she cut up several tomatoes, mushrooms, and some cabbage. Deciding it needed some extra flavor she sprinkled some dried fennel leaves into it. Giving Proetus a large portion on one of the salvaged plates, she served herself enough for dinner. As soon as she handed the plate to Proetus he used his hands to eat. The speed in which he was eating at let her know that he was very hungry.

He stopped eating for a moment before declaring, "It is delicious."

"Thank you." She replied before she started to eat.

She did have to admit that adding the fennel was a nice touch. It made the eggs taste much better. After she finished eating she set her plate aside. Proetus had finished eating and was holding his plate.

"Do you have anything else to eat?" He asked.

It was more than a little surprising how hungry he was but she did remember that her father and brother used to eat much more food than she or her sisters ever did.

Medusa answered by saying. "I do have some dried fish."

"Could I have some please? I am famished."

As she stood she took his plate and responded, "Sure."

She brought his plate over to where she had the fish drying. After take a few pieces she brought them to her one kettle and cooked them over the open flame. Once she was done cooking she smothered her fire with dirt. She did not want anyone to spot the fire so she usually kept them burning very briefly. Placing the plate in his hands she sat back down in her chair. He ate the fish just as greedily as he did the eggs and was done in no time. Medusa noticed that the sun had already begun setting. It dawned on her that if she tried to take him to the village this late they might get lost. She was stuck with him until tomorrow morning.

He interrupted his thoughts by asking, "That was delicious, where did you learn to make eggs like that."

"I just tried different things until I found something I liked." She answered.

After brief moment he nodded.

She was very curious to find out how he ended up in the forest so she asked, "How did you end up alone and lost?"

"It is a long story." He told her.

"Well I was thinking that it is too late to take you safely to the village. First thing tomorrow morning I will take you."

"So we have time for my story." He said with a chuckle.

"Yes."

"Well…" He started with a long pause before continuing, "I am from the city of Argos and we are currently involved in a war with Sparta. I was part of a naval fleet looking to flank the Spartans. Unfortunately they were prepared for the maneuver and met us off the coast of this island. My ship was hit by flaming oil, part of which struck my face and knocked me overboard. I was dragged ashore by someone from the ship. Sadly I believe they died from their wounds but there is no way for me to know for sure since I was blinded. I wandered for a bit on a beach and eventually was discovered by a small merchant group. A few days ago I was accidentally separated from them and have been wandering lost since. I thank the gods that I found you or I surely would have died."

His story made sense to her based on how he was dressed and his wounds. She still had a several lack of trust for him.

Deciding it was best to learn more about him she asked, "What work did you do in Argos? Where you a soldier?"

Her question brought laughter in response.

Once he calmed down he stated, "Not quite. I am the son of Abas, King of Argos."

Medusa was immediately impressed. She had no realized that she was dealing with royalty. No doubt he would be in a hurry to head back to Argos.

She told him, "Well I will get you to the village. I am certain they will help you find your way to Sami so you can return home."

"Ahh, so this is Kefalonia. I was unsure which island I had ended up on."

"Yes."

His face shifted to sadness before he declared, "I am not so sure I will be welcomed back."

Medusa was very confused so she asked, "Why?"

"My father had recently passed away which left my twin brother Acrisius and I in a dispute over the rule of Argos. Without my sight I will be powerless to stop him from attaining the throne. I would probably be better off not going back. He is likely to slay me in my current condition."

Medusa frowned. She had no idea of anything happening outside of the limited scope of her existence and this all seemed quite dangerous.

"So what will do you?" She asked out of curiosity.

"I have nowhere else to go. I shall return home even though it is likely a death sentence."

"What about your family?"

"I had been engaged to a woman but before our marriage I was to deal with the Spartans to prove my worthiness to become the King."

There was a long uncomfortable pause before he finally asked, "And what of you Medusa?"

"What do you mean?"

"How did you manage to be living in these woods in a cave?"

That was a subject that she was very hesitant to answer directly.

Pausing to think of something to say she just decided to tell him a lie, "I am an orphan and I had nowhere else to go."

She felt slightly bad about telling him a lie but she was certain if he knew that she was a hideous monster he would either flee or attack her. It was not something that she could risk.

Proetus stated, "Life is sometimes hard. I was quite fortunate to be born in the family I am part of. I was hoping to use my new position to improve the life of my people but my brother's greed and selfishness were uncontrollable. He had always been selfish and did not seem to care for my father's lessons. I fear that he will drive Argos to ruin but a blind man can do nothing."

He seemed quite sad as he sighed deeply. It was obvious that whatever was going on with him weighed on him heavily.

After a slight moment he seemed to shake himself out of his malaise before he asked, "How long have you been living out here?"

Thinking on it she realized that she was not entirely sure. She guessed it was about five years.

Answering his question she said, "About five years."

"All alone?"

"You are the first person to come here."

"I hear chicken and after eating eggs for dinner I suspect you have several. You served me fresh vegetables and fish so I guess you either steal a lot of vegetables or have your own garden."

“I have my own garden. I have ten chicken and there is a village on the coast where they let anyone use the nets to catch their own fish.”

“Quite the survivor.”

She could tell from his facial expression and tone of voice that he was being sincere in his compliment.

“Medusa I am quite tired. Do you have something I could sleep on? Maybe a blanket I could use as well.”

“Of course.”

She was not going to let the man sleep on her bed but she saw no problem letting him use some blankets on the ground in the dry cave. She stood and guided him into the cave and after releasing him she collected a pair of blankets. Setting one down on the ground she helped him sit down. He removed his sandals, his leather tunic and finally his chiton leaving him only wearing a perizoma. She passed him the blanket. As he took it and slowly spread it out he laid down.

Proetus then said to her, “Thank you once again.”

“You are welcome.”

Normally she would have slipped off her chiton before going to bed but with a man nearby she felt more comfortable with it on. She chuckled at herself over her own modesty. He could not see her either way. Sitting on her bed she removed her sandals and then laid down. While lying there she heard his slow and even breathing. It was obvious that he fell asleep almost instantly. It took her a long time before she could finally fall asleep.

CHAPTER 15

Once again Georgios loudly woke Medusa from her sleep. She laid on her bed for a moment before remembering that a blind man named Proetus was sleeping on the floor. She quickly sat up and looked over where he was sleeping. He was still lying on the blanket that she had set down. His eyes were open.

He must have heard her sit up because he immediately asked quietly, "Medusa are you awake?"

She blushed. His hearing was sharp because she was certain that she did not make any noise sitting up.

Softly she replied to him, "Yes."

"I hope you slept well." He stated.

"Thank you, I did."

He sat up before declaring, "For a cave it sure is nice here."

She chuckled at his comment before stating, "It is. When there are rainstorms it does not get wet in here. Also it never gets too hot or too cold."

"How big is it in here?" He asked.

"About the size of a large bedroom like my father's."

"Your father?"

She flushed. She forgot that she was trying to keep things to herself.

Trapped by her own mistake she admitted, "Yes my father. I used to live in a town called Pireaus."

"I know it. It is a port for Athens."

"Yes."

"How did you end up here?"

She was not willing to tell him the truth so she quickly lied, "When my parents died I wandered for some time before finding my way here. I had nothing and knew no one so when I found this cave I set it up as a home."

It was a handy lie and she was quite happy to have thought of it so easily.

"Ahh." He said.

They sat there quietly for a moment awkwardly before Medusa stated, "I guess I should make us breakfast."

"I cannot tell you how much I appreciate all of your help."

"It is no problem." She told him before standing up and stretching.

As she slipped on her sandals she heard Georgios squawk again. He was probably hungry. She chuckled at him.

"What are you laughing about?" Proetus asked.

"Georgios."

"Who is Georgios?"

She blushed yet again before answering, "He is my rooster."

"Oh. He is the one who so loudly woke us up this morning."

"Yes. Every morning he does that."

"Always helpful when you have work in the morning."

"Very true. I have to feed the chicken before I cook breakfast. They get very fussy if I collect their eggs and they have not eaten."

"Alright. I will get dressed."

She strolled past him and picked up her bucket. After sprinkling some grain for her chicken she set the bucket down and collected several eggs. She set them aside before collecting some vegetables. This time she decided to cook some pieces of fish into the eggs with the vegetables. After getting everything ready she started a fire.

"Medusa!" Proetus' voice called out from the cave.

"Yes?"

"Could you help me out please?"

"Sure." Medusa responded before setting down her pot and walking into the cave.

Proetus was standing in his perizoma flailing his hands about apparently searching for something. She guessed that it was probably his clothing. Sitting off to the side she spotted his chiton and sandals. She bent down and collected them before setting them in his hands.

"Thank you. I was having trouble finding them."

She turned back around and headed back to working on cooking breakfast. It did not take long and as she finished Proetus came stumbling out. She felt horrible for him as it was clear that he really was blind. His arms were outstretched as he seemed to be grasping for something. After a moment she realized he was searching for the chair that he had sat in the evening before. She set down her spoon she was stirring the food with and helped guide him to the chair. After he was settled, she finished making breakfast. It was smelling wonderful as she cooked it. Once it was finished she brought a plate of it to Proetus to eat and then sat down with her plate. It tasted just as good as it smelled.

"It is delicious." Proetus told her.

"Thank you."

He nodded. She found it awkward whenever he spoke or made a gesture towards her. He was clearly talking to her or gesturing at her but generally he was slightly off. It was almost as though he was nodding to a person standing next to her. She felt bad for him.

Curiosity struck her so she asked, "Does it hurt?"

"What?"

"Your eyes?"

He paused and looked thoughtful for a moment before continuing, "At first it was extremely painful. It hurt for some time before scabbing over. Then it itched. Now I feel nothing."

Something made her very curious to examine his eyes closer. She stood up and moved closer so she could see.

He suddenly asked, "What are you doing?"

She felt heat from blushing rise on her face.

"Sorry, I just wanted to see your eyes."

"What do they look like?" He asked curiously.

"White, almost milky." She told him.

Sullenly he stated, "Oh, I was right."

"Right?"

"Yes. I cannot go home. My brother will take advantage of my blindness, likely even just have me killed."

She frowned. It was her plan to send him home but she knew that she could not do so if he would be killed. Maybe someone in the village could help him although she was not sure about that either. The people in the village were very poor and would struggle to care for a blind man on top of their own burdens.

Proetus stood up and asked, "Would it be possible to get some water?"

Normally Medusa kept a clay pitcher filled with water but she forgot to fill it at the pond yesterday so it was empty.

She told him, "We will have to go to the pond. I am afraid that I used the last of it last night."

"That is fine. Could you take me? I think I could use a bath as well. It has been some time and I can smell myself."

Seeing nothing wrong with letting him bathe she responded, "Sure, let me get something for you to dry yourself off once you finish."

After grabbing one of her clean woolen blankets, a himation, the bag she used for plenty of things, and her coin purse she strolled over to Proetus. Reaching out she tenderly took his hand. It was then that she was hit with a sudden sense of nervousness. It was probably the first time in her life that she was so close to a man who was not a relative or not trying to harm her. He was looking in her direction and he smiled as he held her hand. Lightly tugging she guided him towards the pond.

As they walked Proetus asked, "What sort of things do you do to pass the time out here?"

Without thinking she answered, "Outside of working to get food I spend a lot of time chasing down Anthousa."

"Anthousa?"

Laughing loudly she stated, "One of my hens. She is always escaping the pen."

He chuckled at her answer before saying, "When I was young I was tasked with managing my father's ranch where he kept herds of goat and sheep. We were constantly dealing with runaways. It really is amazing how devilishly sneaky unintelligent animals are."

"Yes it is. I was in the middle of collecting parts to rebuild the pen to be sturdier when I ran into you."

"I would be more than willing to help you. I cannot see but I am still capable."

Medusa turned to examine him for a moment. He did indeed look quite strong. Pushing the wooden posts into the ground would be very difficult for her but he could probably do it easily enough.

"What else did you do with your time? Surely foraging for food and chasing a chicken is not everything."

"I have been trying to teach myself how to play a lyre I found in an abandoned home."

"Wonderful. The lyre is my favorite instrument. My mother played it quite well."

She frowned. The way he stated it made it seem as though his mother was dead as well. Not being able to think of anything appropriate to say she said nothing. They arrived at the pond.

"We are here." She declared.

"I can hear a waterfall."

"Yes, we are next to a cliff-side that has a waterfall which pours into a pool. It turns into a small river that heads out to the edge of the forest."

Solemnly he stated, "It sounds beautiful."

A small pang of guilt struck her because it was beautiful and he could not see it.

"It is. I will set this blanket down here and let you bathe. Just call me when you are ready to go back to the cave."

"Alright. Thank you." He said before releasing his hold on her and bending over to remove his sandals.

Medusa started walking away. As she got past the first few trees she found herself suddenly very curious so she turned around and moved behind a tree to watch him. A swell of nervousness hit her as he removed his chiton. It was then that she finally took time to admire his form. He was slender with a muscular build and she thought that he was very attractive. Every part of his body was lean and toned. While she had no idea what sort of fitness regimen a soldier would have she suspected that it was probably quite intense. After all, they had to be able to run and fight for long periods of time. At least that is what her father once said about her cousin. Her cousin was not this fit though. With a feeling that she could only describe as lust, she eagerly watched him slowly work his way into the water. He made his way over to the waterfall. Once there he turned his head upwards to let the water run over him. She had done the same thing many times before and imagined it probably felt wonderful for him as it did for her. After a bit of time letting the water run over him, he moved back to the shore. He stopped when he got in the middle but froze. She thought that maybe he might have heard her but she swore that she did not so much as move a muscle. Her heart was beating so fast that she swore she could hear it echoing.

Suddenly he called out, "Medusa!"

Part of her wanted to run out of embarrassment. He must have realized that she was watching him.

Deciding to play it off she waited a while before calling out, "Yes?"

He must have believed that she was a bit away because he yelled out, "Could you guide me to my clothes? I got kind of lost. All you need to do is line me up with them and then I will be able to find them."

Stepping out she walked forward. She looked back where his clothes were and then strolled over to them.

Once she was standing by them she announced, "I am right by your clothes. You need to walk to my voice."

He flushed lightly before saying, "Well. I doubt you want to see me naked so you can leave."

She chuckled to herself because she had already seen him naked and honestly she wanted to see more.

"Alright." She told him before walking away.

Once again, as soon as she got out of sight she turned back around to watch him. She had no idea why she had such an overwhelming desire to see more but she did. It was probably a bit evil to take advantage of a blind man but she shrugged that off. Keeping as quiet as she could she watched him step out cautiously while grasping downward until he fumbled into the blanket that she left for him. He dried himself off before getting dressed.

Finally he called out, "Medusa I am ready if you could come back."

Waiting a few moments she finally stood up and walked over to him. As she reached out to let him hold her arm she took another moment to admire his form. Even dressed in his chiton she had to admit he was pleasant on the eyes.

He tenderly took her arm before saying, "That was probably the best bath I have had in a long time."

Me too, she thought evilly to herself.

"That is good." She told him.

"So what is the plan now?" He asked her.

"I am going to take you to the village. However I was wondering if you could help me with something beforehand?"

"Of course. I would love to help you with all that you have done for me. What do you need?" He replied to her in what seemed to be a very sincere tone.

"I have to go buy some posts for my chicken's pen and I need help carrying them back home before I push them into the ground."

"And you need my muscles."

"Well you have so many I thought you would not mind letting me use them."

He laughed and said in what seemed almost a flirty tone, "I would love to let you use my muscles."

Heat rose to her face from a blush.

They continued walking for a bit a before she stated, "We can stop at a place to buy the posts and then put them in before heading to the village."

"Okay. I have nothing better to do."

She nodded at him. Using her free hand she pulled her himation off of her shoulder before wrapping it around her head. They continued walking for some time before finally arriving at the pathway outside the village. Glancing where the man from the village had told her was someone selling wood she spotted a larger home with another half building next to it. Outside of the half building was large stacks of wood. There was no doubt that the man was harvesting the trees on the outskirt of the forest that she lived in. It was a good thing for her that she lived so far in that it would take a long time to ever get to her from cutting down trees.

"This way." She told Proetus before heading towards the home.

CHAPTER 16

As they approached the house she spotted several men working in the half building. They all had either an axe or a long knife and were working with various lengths of wood. All of the men had heavily tanned skin, no doubt from working in the sun all the time, and were wearing nothing but leather skirts. Standing nearby was an older man who she was certain was supervising the younger men. The old man was wearing a full chiton. He turned to look at them as Medusa approached with Proetus. The man took an unusual double take when he saw the injuries on Proetus' face.

In order to spare Proetus any embarrassment she quickly said, "Hello. I need to see about buying ten or so wood posts for a chicken pen."

The old man shifted to look at her. She made sure to keep her face pointing downwards to ensure the man could not look into her eyes.

"Ahh. When do you need them?" The old man smoothly asked her.

"Immediately. My chicken keep escaping."

"Oh… That could be quite difficult to do as we have another order for firewood. It is still a bit away from the colder season but people from Poulata like to stock dry wood beforehand."

Medusa got more than a little frustrated but before she could say anything Proetus stated, "How much will it cost to convince you to make her posts immediately?"

Turning back to Proetus the old man answered, "Two drachma for the wood and another to rush the posts. Our other orders can wait with proper financial compensation."

"Agreed." Proetus responded before pulling out his own coin purse.

He released his grasp on Medusa's forearm and clumsily fumbled through his purse to pull out three silver drachma.

As he passed them to the man Medusa whispered to him, "You do not need to pay for my posts. I can pay myself."

Turning to face her he grinned before saying, "It is the least that I could do for all you have done for me. Please let me pay."

Medusa surrendered. She saw no reason to fight over something as silly as a few silver coins.

"Okay." She told him.

After paying the man he grasped out with his hand, a hint that he wanted to retake her forearm, so she reached her arm out and let him grasp a hold of her arm. He squeezed her forearm softly a few times before turning back towards the man.

The old man pocketed the three drachma as he announced, "We should have your posts ready just after lunch. About how tall do you want the posts to be?"

Raising her free hand up to her waist she told him, "Up to my waist please."

"Easy enough. I shall see you both after lunch."

"Thank you." Medusa told him before guiding Proetus away.

"Where shall we go while we wait?" Proetus asked.

"The only thing around us is the Poulata."

"I suppose we should go there."

"Maybe someone there might be able to help you find your way back to Argos."

His face shifted to a solemn expression before he softly stated, "I have decided not to go back there."

"Oh."

"Without my vision I would find myself heading to my death."

"Where will you go then?" She cautiously asked.

She did not want to admit it but she was almost hoping that he would want to stay with her. Although she thought that he would probably be repelled if he knew the reality of what she was. A hideous monster.

He responded, "I do not know but I am sure something worthwhile will come along."

For some reason she got it in her head that he was talking about her. Maybe it was her own loneliness speaking. She had spent years virtually alone and just in the brief time Proetus stumbled into her she had found herself glad for the company. The walk to the village was quite brief.

As they entered she asked, "Are you hungry? One booth here sells fresh fruits and cooked lamb."

"I would love some lamb." He told her.

Guiding him over to one of the booths she bought both of them some lamb ribs. She rarely got to eat lamb so she savored it quite a bit. Glancing at him she could tell that he enjoyed his as well since he was attacking it voraciously.

The man who had sold Medusa her baskets and the bucket approached them from behind before stating, "Young man you are new here."

As Proetus turned towards the man. The man responded by having a shocked look on his face. She realized that he was surprised by the scars on Proetus' face. She was glad that Proetus could not see his reaction.

Proetus responded, "Yes. It is my first time here. I was curious if you knew anyone who could help a blind man. I find myself without a place to stay or work to do."

The old man frowned at Proetus before stating, "Honestly friend we are all quite poor and I doubt anyone has the ability to feed another mouth, especially a blind person."

Medusa was shocked at his forthrightness. She had expected a more polite rejection, of course she did not know the people here that well.

Before she could recover from her shock Proetus stated, "I understand. I am both young and healthy but I can see the difficulty. I am certain I will find my way somehow. Thank you."

She was very conflicted about the answer of the old man. Part of her wanted to be left alone but another part of her was starting to greatly enjoy Proetus' company.

He turned towards her and asked, "What else do they have for sale?"

"Not too much just basic food and items someone might need to maintain their home."

"Makes sense. It reminds me of a small village on our island not far from where Argos lies."

Curious to learn more about him she said, "Tell me about it."

Giving her a smile he responded, "It is called Alea and my father had a small hunting base where we would go before the winter to hunt wild animals. I remember the fun we would have chasing down wild boar and just about anything else that we could find. It was the best of times for my family. Especially between me and my brother."

"What happened to him?" Medusa asked before realizing it was not her place to ask such a personal question.

If she offended him by the question he did not show it as it as he immediately responded, "Power. He became obsessed with power and even before my father finally died he was jockeying position to attempt to remove me. Thankfully my years of service in the military had allowed me to have a close alliance with the Argive military."

After a long uncomfortable pause he finally continued, "But that is all the past. I must find myself a new future."

She had no answer to his statement. Unlike her, he probably had some sort of future. She suspected that her future was to hide in her cave until she died. What else could a hideous monster do? She asked herself.

"And what of you Medusa?" He asked.

"What do you mean?"

He grinned before responding, "What are your plans?"

"Just keep doing what I am doing. Learn how to play my lyre. Finally catch one of those hare for a stew."

"Hare?"

"Yes, they are small fluffy creatures that run wild in the forest along the border of the farms. I heard that they taste wonderful in stew but I have yet to be able to catch one with my stick."

Proetus laughed heartily. She was very confused as to why he was laughing.

Finally he told her, "A stick would never work to catch a hare. They are just too fast for even the most nimble of hunter to get close enough to hit them with it. You need a bow and arrow to succeed."

"Oh." She sullenly stated.

"It looks like another thing I must help you with before heading out."

"That is not necessary." She told him.

Shaking his head Proetus stated, "You saved my life. The least I could do is help you by making a bow and teaching you how to do it."

"You do not have to." She insisted.

Of course she did not want to admit it but she was more than happy to spend additional time with him.

"I insist. I am not in a huge hurry to head off to Sami but I am thinking it might be my only option. I highly doubt any other village on this island have much need for a blind man."

"Well I guess it would not hurt. If a bow could help me kill a hare I am willing to try it."

"It is decided. Let us ask the people here if anyone sells some sinew. I am confident we can get the wooden bow from our friends who are making the posts."

"Sinew?"

"Yes. You can use ligaments from animals to make the string for a bow."

She understood.

"We can ask around." She told him.

They bounced to a few booths before coming to the man who sold her the bucket and baskets. She should have guessed that he would have been their best option. He had a long stretch of very disgusting piece of random part of an animal. After tucking it into her bag and paying the man they headed back to the home where her posts where being made.

As they strolled along Proetus stated, "The sun feels wonderful on my face. I think that it is beautiful out today."

Glancing up into the sky she noted that it was indeed lovely outside. She rarely paid attention to the weather unless it was raining.

"It is." She told him.

As they approached the house she spotted the old man. He recognized them approaching and scurrying over to them.

Once he got closer he told them, "We just finished your posts. I had them made a little thinner than normal fence posts so you can carry all of them. They are more than sturdy enough for chicken."

Giving him a smile Medusa said, "Thank you sir."

Proetus interrupted, "Sir, do you happen to have a piece of wood I could carve into a bow?"

The old man looked thoughtful for a moment before declaring, "I do. Since you paid so well for the posts I will toss in a piece of wood for that."

"I appreciate it." Proetus stated to him,

The man walked away and after talking with one of his workers he bent down and collected a long stick. The workers picked up 10 wooden posts and strolled over. She could tell that they would work perfectly. The younger man set them down in front of Medusa and Proetus. The older man set down the stick with the posts. She was struggling to figure out how she would carry all of them and guide Proetus.

Almost as if he was reading her mind Proetus said, "Pass them to me. I can carry them while you guide me back home."

The old man and his worker walked away.

"Hold your arms out." Medusa instructed.

Proetus extended his arms. Scooping up one of the posts she set it on his arms.

"Perfect. I can carry all ten of them easily."

She continued stacking the other posts and once she had them all in his arms she set the stick in the pile and then took a hold of his hand to help guide him. As they walked back to the cave she made sure to be extra careful with him so he would not fall. She did not realize it until she entered the forest but that was the first time she did not look back to make sure she was being followed. Something about having a man with her made her feel safe. Unwrapping her himation she flung it over her shoulder.

Proetus commented, “This island seems to have a lot of snakes on it.”

Medusa giggled. He had not realized that it was her snakes.

It was probably best that she not tell him about them so she stated, “It does but they are harmless.”

“That is good to know. Back at Argos we do have snakes and I can only think of ohia as being dangerous.”

“Is it bad?”

“No.” He stated.

She noticed that as they walked they were almost there. Of course silly Anthousa had once again escaped.

“Anthousa!” Medusa called out.

“Did she escape again?”

Chuckling at him she answered, “Yes. I think I can see her over by the chairs.”

He laughed before stating, “She really is a trouble maker.”

“Which is why I need to rebuild my pen.”

“Very well. Let us get to work. I need to earn my keep.”

She slowly removed the stick and posts from his arms until all of them except one where not neatly stacked on the ground.

He shifted the post from his arm to his right hand before asking, “Where do you want the first one?”

Giving a grin she reached out to grab his free hand. Slowly she directed him to a spot next to one of the old posts. She decided to extend the size of the chicken pen by a little bit. As she set his post exactly where she wanted it he began to push it into the ground. The men who made the post did a wonderful job because she had not noticed it initially but they sharpened one end of the post so it could be easily pushed into the ground. Proetus strained for a moment as he forced the post in.

Once he stopped he wiggled the post before declaring, “I believe that is perfect.”

Taking a moment to examine it she decided that he was right. It looked like it was not going to fall over from either wild chicken trying to escape or the winter weather of the island.

"Next one?" Proetus asked.

She chuckled before passing him the next one and then guiding him where she wanted it. One by one she walked him through setting up all of the posts.

After they were all done she told him, "Sit down and relax I am going to pull apart these baskets and make the weaving into the fence for the pen."

"Alright. Could you guide me?"

"Yes." She told him before helping him to sit down.

After he was sitting she collected her baskets and then sat down on the ground next to him. Slowly but surely she began to disassemble each basket. As she went she casually snuck a peek at him. She was finding him more and more handsome as she continued to learn about him. It concerned her greatly.

CHAPTER 17

Medusa continued to slowly take apart the baskets. She was confident that once the thin pieces of wood from these baskets were wrapped around the posts they would keep her silly chicken from making their escape. Well, keep Anthousa from escaping. The rest of them were very well behaved.

"Medusa, can I ask you something?" Proetus said while interrupting her wandering mind.

She saw no issue with a question so she said, "Sure."

"What do you look like?"

Panic slipped through her. The last thing she wanted to do was to let him find out that she was a hideous monster with green skin and snakes for hair.

After a long pause he said, "Medusa?"

"Sorry. I think it is hard to describe me. I do have blue eyes and my skin is not quite like everyone else's."

"Can I see?"

She was confused. How could he see her face he was blind!

"How can you see me?" She asked.

"I can touch your face to get an idea of what you look like."

Full panic hit her. If he touched her face and accidentally touched the snakes he would know something was wrong. Looking to her left and right she tried to figure what to do to escape her newest dilemma. Sitting on her chair was one of her himation. An idea struck her. She could wrap it around her head by her ears to cover up the snakes and keep him from feeling them.

"Sure." She told him as she stood up.

Moving over to the chair she grabbed the himation and wrapped it around the snakes to contain them behind her head. Spinning the himation she made sure that it would sit in place and not slip off her head. She moved over to Proetus and knelt in front of him so that her face was just out of reach of his hands. Tenderly taking his hands she placed them on her cheeks. His face lit up with a smile as he began softly touching her face. He moved from her cheeks to her chin and then slowly along her face. His hands stopped when they made contact with her himation before moving them away.

"Your face feels beautiful to me."

Her face got warm as she felt a twinge of embarrassment.

"Thank you." She responded as she stood and moved back over to her basket.

Relief over the fact her himation worked to keep him from touching those foul snakes ripped through her. The last thing that she could handle was this man fleeing in horror from finding out what she really was. She began working on the baskets. At this point she only had two baskets left and as she unweaved them she took another moment to look at Proetus. The thought that it was an insane stroke of luck that she found the one man out there who would be immune to her curse struck her. A little part of her hoped that maybe her luck had finally begun to change.

As she finished the last basket she asked, "What would you like for dinner? I can make more eggs or I have some fish left."

Giving a chuckle her stated, "We need to make that bow so we can increase your options."

"Yes." She stated.

"Let us go with fish."

As she stood up she said, "Alright. I need to wash my hands and get some more water. Once I get back I will make dinner."

"I will be here." Proetus replied with a chuckle.

She dusted off her chiton before spinning around and grabbing the jar that she kept water in. Her walk to the pond was uneventful and before long she was back at the cave cooking. After picking some vegetables she realized that she was going to need to expand her garden if Proetus stayed much longer. She was not a heavy eater but he ate almost double what she did.

As she set the plate of fish and fried vegetables in his hands Proetus stated, "Tonight we can make your bow. Do you have anything sharper than the knives you cook with?"

Pausing for a moment to think on it she remembered the sword that she took from the men who tried to assault her in Athens.

"Yes, I have an old sword that I found." She told him.

"Can I see it?" He asked before pausing and chuckling.

He then continued, "Well, not so much see as hold I guess."

She giggled at his joke. Even blinded he seemed to have a sense of humor about him.

"Sure." She told him as she went into her cave.

The sword was sitting up against a wall so she picked it up and brought it to him. As she took his plate from his hands she set the sword in his open right hand with the sharp end away from him. He swapped the sword from his right hand to his left and then used his right hand to slowly touch the sword, almost as tenderly as he had touched her face.

He ran a finger along the edge of the sword before stating, "This will work for what we need."

Bending to his right he set the sword down on the ground and then asked, "May I have my plate back please?"

"Of course." She told him as she gave it back to him.

He grinned at her. Next she served herself dinner and sat down in the other chair to eat. She enjoyed her simple meal. After she finished eating she took Proetus' plate and set them aside to clean later.

"Pass me the stick that we bought." Proetus instructed her.

She found the stick and passed it to him.

"I am going to go wash these plates." She told him.

"Alright. I will get started on carving this bow. Could you kindly collect a handful of as straight as possible sticks as well?"

"Oh course!" She told him joyfully.

After picking up the dishes that needed to be washed she headed off to the pond. She knelt down next to the pond and washing off the debris on each plate. After she finished she decided to put the plates away before searching the forest for sticks. Her search for sticks was pretty successful and she found ten of them. As she walked back up to the cave she spotted Proetus working diligently on the bow. He was carving the edges into a point with divot on the point. He had also skimmed down the stick itself a bit and made it very smooth looking.

"Did you find any sticks?" He asked as she approached.

"I found ten that appear straight."

"May I see them please?"

"See?" She answered with a chuckle.

Giving out a wild laugh he retorted, "A figure of speech."

He set down the sword and bow before gesturing for her to hand him the sticks. As she passed him the sticks their hands brushed and she felt a rush of nervousness. She was suffering from delusions of attraction. Especially since he would undoubtedly run as fast as he could if he discovered what she really was.

Interrupting her train of thought Proetus stated, "These sticks are perfect. Could you take a few and peel off every branch for me?"

"Of course!" She responded happily as she picked up one of the sticks.

"Be careful not to tear into the branch itself. We need it to be smooth and straight as possible for it to be an arrow."

"Alright."

She worked as carefully as possible to peel off the leaves and small branches that were attached to each stick. Once she had all of them done she set her pile down on the ones that Proetus had completed.

"Next I need to stretch and dry the sinew we bought. Could you pass it to me?"

"Of course." She stood and collected up the very gross sinew from the bag.

Proetus fiddled with it and stretched it out before threading it into the ends of the new bow. He continued to run his hands along it until it seemed as though it was now a very tight thin string.

"Could you pass me some cloth to rub it? I need to remove as much moisture from it as possible."

She handed him an old rag that she had resting on the arm of her chair.

He rubbed it rapidly as he could for a while before declaring, "It should be ready by tomorrow morning for our hunt."

Next, he picked up one of the sticks and the sword. Slowly and evenly he used the sword to peel the bark off of the stick and then smooth it out. Taking the edge of the sword he sharpened the stick to a point on one end and then carved a notch on the other end. Medusa sat quietly watching him work. He made his way through each stick until all ten of them were complete.

As he rested the sword on the ground he said, "We are ready as we can be. Tomorrow I will have to teach you how to shoot a bow and then we hunt. I imagine once we kill a hare the stew will taste as wonderful as everything else you have made."

She smiled at his inserted compliment about her cooking.

"I hope so." She stated.

"Let us get some rest for tomorrow." He declared.

Standing up she went back into the cave and pulled out one of her blankets. As she slowly spread it out for him she wished that she could share a bed with him. It was not the thoughts of a lady and she would never dare speak it to him but it did cross her mind. He slowly walked into the cave with his arms flailing out to attempt to help him avoid hitting anything. She took his hand and guided him to the spot where the blanket on the ground was resting.

As he knelt down he sat on the blanket and said, "Thank you for the help. I am slowly learning where everything is."

Grinning at him she commented, "That is good."

Fiddling with his sandals he removed them before lifting his chiton over his head. She knelt down and rested a hand on his shoulder to help guide him backwards. Once he was lying down she took a second blanket and spread it out over him.

He gave her a smile as he stated, "Sleep well Medusa."

"You as well." She told him before strolling over to her own bed and sitting down on it.

She removed her sandals and then spread out on the bed. She struggled some time to sleep as she daydreamed about Proetus. Finally she was able to sleep.

* * * * *

Medusa startled awake on her own to see that the sun had not quite rose. She could hear Proetus' deep and even breathing. He was still soundly sleeping. She sat up and looked over at him. He was resting on his back with the blanket that she had placed on him still there. Attempting to sleep again she rested her head back on the bed. It was of no avail. Thoughts about Proetus had distracted her. Deciding it was best to give up and do something else with her time she got out of bed. Sneaking as quietly as she could, she slipped past him and stepped outside the cave. Her chicken startled by her movement and responded excitedly to her picking up the bucket. She sprinkled grain for them to eat. It was not possible to examine her garden until the sun rose so she decided to go take a bath. She grabbed a clean chiton and an extra blanket to dry herself before heading off to the pond. It was a bit harder to see in the dark but she made her way to the pond in one piece. After setting down the blanket and clean chiton she reached out to touch the water in the pond. It was cold. Back when she lived in Piraeus she was so spoiled with having warm water available to bathe. The idea that she would someday live in a cave and bathe in a cold pond would have never crossed her mind. Sighing heavily she chased the thoughts of the past out of her head before slipping off her chiton. Later in the day, after she went to hunt hare, she was going to have to hand wash her dirty chiton and extra blankets. It dawned on her that she would have to sneak out again and sheer more wool from wandering sheep. With Proetus here she was going to run out of clean blankets. Also she considered making him a new chiton as well. Slowly she unwrapped her chest and then removed her perizoma.

As she dipped a toe into the water she grumpily said, "Cold."

Gritting her teeth she stepped into the pond and then slowly made her way deeper in. It was so cold that her body was immediately peppered with small bumps. Closing her eyes, she dipped her whole body into the pond. Cold water splashed over her as she rose up. Her teeth chattered from the cold water. She carried on by dipping into the water and rubbing her hands down her arms and sides in order to clean herself. Medusa wished that she had access to pumice and her strigil to clean herself but all of her searching on the island had left her without either. It was just going to have to be cold water as her only option. She dipped her head once again into the water. Something of note that she had not realized when she was first cursed was the fact that she seemed more capable of holding her breath much longer than before. There was no reason that she could think of other than maybe the snakes on her head must have breathed for her. Testing that theory she kept her head down under the water as long as she could. She could feel the ugly snakes on her head moving to the surface. They were clearly part of her in more ways that just being hair. Finally giving up holding her breath, she rose out of the water and chuckled.

A voice in the dark that she immediately recognized as Proetus called out, "Medusa?"

CHAPTER 18

Medusa let out a small panicked squeak and then covered her chest with her arms. She was bare naked and he was standing near the edge of the pond!

"There you are." Proetus stated.

Her face flushed a heated red out of embarrassment.

"What are you doing? I heard you leaving but it took me a while to catch up with you."

"I am bathing!" She exclaimed huffily.

"Oh… I did hear some water splashing but I did not know what it was."

Her panic passed over her when she remembered that he was blind. It was very uncomfortable to be standing naked in front of a man that she barely knew but at least she knew he could not see her. Modesty was something her mother had taught all of her daughters.

After she recovered from her initial shock she told him, "It was me. You were sleeping so I thought it was a good time to bathe."

"I apologize for interrupting. I believe I can find my way back to your cave."

She was concerned with how a blind man would find his way back so she asked, "How can you? You are blind."

Giving a chuckle he told her, "I counted my steps as I walked this way. It was thirty one steps so all I have to do is turn around and walk thirty one steps back while dodging trees."

Not wanting him to get lost she told him, "If you wait a moment I can walk you back."

"I will be fine." He stated as he started to turn around.

Right as he started to turn around he slipped on something and tumbled sideways into the pond! She heard him call out in shock before being submerged in the water.

"Proetus!" She called out as she stepped quickly towards where he fell.

When she got to where he had fallen in she reached down into the water and felt his shoulder underwater. It was unusual that he was still underwater since the pond was not very deep where he fell. She was worried that he might have been hurt and when she pulled as hard as she could to get his head above water she saw he had a bruise that formed on his forehead. It took all of her strength to drag him above the water while trying to move him out of the pond. Utterly exhausted from dragging him she collapsed on top of him. It was then that he recovered and coughed roughly. Medusa realized at that exact moment that when she collapsed on him she had done so completely naked! Moving as quickly as she could, she scurried off of him and on to her rear right next to him.

He continued coughing for a moment before recovering enough to say, "It seems I have to thank you yet again."

"You are welcome." She stated.

Giving a chuckle he stated, "And now all of my clothing is wet and I believe I am covered in mud."

Taking a moment to look at him she noted that he was right. She too had mud all over herself from dragging him out of the pond. He sat up and groaned out lightly.

"Are you well?" She asked him.

"Yes, I struck my head when I fell however I am fine as it only hurts a little."

She needed to rinse off all of the mud so she stood up. Proetus must have heard her stand because he climbed off of his feet as well. As she started to step back into the pond she watched him strip off all of his clothing and then start to walk into the pond.

"What are you doing?" She asked him nervously.

"I am going to rinse off this mud and then try to wash my clothing."

From a bit of a distance away she watched him walk into the pond. He dipped his chiton into the water and squeezed it several times in an attempt to clean it. She was probably watching him entirely too closely as he splashed water on himself. Absentmindedly she rubbed the mud off of her body. He turned away and started to head out of the pond. On his back was still a streak of mud which she guessed that he missed.

"You still have mud on your back." She informed him.

Giving out a chuckle he stated, "I will get it."

He backed into the pond and then submerged himself to try and rinse the mud off. As he stood she saw that he failed.

"Did I get it?" He asked.

"No."

"Could you help me please?"

Her voice cracked as she answered, "Of course."

With his back still turned towards her, she cautiously stepped closer and after scooping some water, she brought her hand up to the point between his shoulders where mud was still caked. Her hands trembled as she touched him. His back was all muscle and quite firm. Of all the stories that she heard from her sisters about what a man should be Proetus seemed to fulfill. She made sure to keep her distance in case he turned on her. From the moment she left her home she learned to fear strangers, especially men. Slowly and evenly she dipped her hand in the pond and used the water to rinse off the mud. Medusa did not know how it happened but as she cleaned the mud off she somehow ended up pressed up against him with her free hand on his left shoulder. His skin felt wonderful against hers and wild thoughts of some sort of relationship with him crossed her mind.

Finally his back was clear so she stepped away from him and stated, "There you go."

Proetus turned back towards her as he stated whimsically, "You must be getting tired of me thanking you all the time."

Medusa laughed. Right as he was fully facing her and so close she saw that he had some mud on the side of his face. She scooped some water into her hand and used it to gently rub away the mud. His face shifted to a grin as she cleaned off the mud.

As she dipped her hand for more water Proetus said to her, "You are very kind Medusa."

While rubbing the last of the mud off his cheek she responded, "Thank you."

She wanted nothing more than to leap into his arms and kiss him but fear of him finding out what she really was stopped her.

Proetus interrupted her thoughts by stating, "Shall we head back? I will need to teach you how to use the bow before we go hunt hare."

"Yes." She meekly replied.

"Could you help me find my way back to dry land?"

Reaching out her hand to clasp his she answered, "Sure."

She paced in front of him and then slowly guided him out of the pond. Letting go of his hand she walked over to her blanket and dried herself off.

Walking closer to Proetus she set the blanket in his hand and stated, "Use this to dry yourself off.

Giving a chuckle he said. "I will have to use it as a wrap until I can dry off my chiton."

"I will dry it off by wringing it out when we get back to the cave."

Proetus began drying himself off with the blanket. For some reason her eyes were drawn to watching him and looking where she should not be looking. She had to forcibly pry her eyes away and collect her own clothing. As quickly as she could she got dressed and then slipped on her sandals. Turning back to Proetus she saw that he was drier and that he wrapped the blanket around his waist. In his left hand he was holding his sopping wet chiton.

"Let me take that." She told him as she took the wet chiton away.

As she guided him towards her cave Medusa reflected on Proetus' complete lack of modesty around her. He seemed to have no issue with stripping off all of his clothing around a woman. She wondered why but could not think of a way to ask him. Maybe the Argives just lived differently than Athenians. Once they got back to the cave Medusa had him sit in a chair before she started to ring out his chiton as tightly as she could. After it was as dry as she could make it she hung it off a nearby branch. It was still a little damp but by the time they finished eating she figured that it would be dry enough for them to go hunting. Next she collected a few eggs and some vegetables. This time she decided to pick a few tomatoes and onions. After dicing each she used her pot to cook them into the eggs and then served breakfast to Proetus. She sat down and then started to eat.

"This tastes wonderful. I like the onions."

"Thank you."

After Proetus finished eating he asked, "Are you ready to learn how to use a bow?"

She had to admit that it sounded quite exciting, especially since it would probably make getting food much easier. Setting her plate down, she stood up. The bow and the arrows that Proetus made were sitting next to his chair. He grabbed them in a fumbling manner before standing up himself.

"I can wear this for a while longer so my chiton can dry before we head out to hunt. Is there any mounts of dirt or something soft we could have you fire the bow at nearby?"

Medusa rubbed her chin to think for a moment. Nothing close by came to mind. The closest thing that she could think of was some old dirt mounds from a tree that fell over long before she had arrived in the forest.

She told him, "I think I know of one."

"Let us head there."

Deciding it might be wise to bring a himation since the tree was closer to the edge of the forest she snatched it up and wrapped it around her head like she had when he touched her face. It was a way to cover the snakes and not smother her while she practiced the bow. She slung her bag over her shoulder before tenderly taking Proetus' hand.

"Shall we head off?" She asked.

"Of course."

It was a bit further of a walk than she initially thought but she was able to find the massive tree that had fallen. It kicked up huge mounds that would make excellent targets.

"We are here." She stated.

"Okay. Have you ever seen someone fire a bow?"

Giving an honest answer she replied, "No."

"That is fine. I will teach you. First take the bow in your right hand and then hold one arrow."

She followed his direction.

"Next, find the notch in the back of the arrow and slide the exact middle of the bowstring into the notch while resting the side of the arrow against the bow."

"Okay." She told him as she did as instructed.

"Alright, let me show you how to hold it."

He stepped right up next to her and after a brief bit of fumbling he got a hold of her hand holding the bow. His other hand touched her arm near her elbow and he guided her arm to raise to bow up to her cheek. A little zing of excitement coursed through her by his closeness.

"Rest the side of the arrow on your cheek close to your eye but not exactly next to it. You will close your left eye and use your right to aim. The goal is to point the arrow directly on the target, pull the string back, and then let go of it. Go ahead and try."

She aimed right in the middle of the mound and then pulled the string back and once she felt ready she let go. The string echoed forward but the arrow just fell out of her hand and onto the ground.

"What happened?" He asked.

"The arrow just fell on the ground." She stated factually.

He laughed before declaring, "I guess my instructions where not very good. Let me show you."

Moving over to her other side he said, "Pick up the arrow and hand it to me."

She passed him the arrow. He moved directly up against her and wrapped his firm arms around her. She was mildly surprised to have him hold her like that but before she could protest he pulled her bow up toward the target and straightened her arm out towards where she was facing.

Next he took the arrow and told her, "Put the arrow in the string of the bow as I instructed before."

She did as he said.

"Now aim at your target."

Moving the bow she aimed at the middle of the dirt pile. He took his free hand and ran it down her arm before sliding her hand a bit upwards to have it touching the front end of the arrow.

"Now pinch the end of the arrow that is in the string and pull it back."

As she did as he told her he brought his face up to her ear and whispered, "Face the target and close your left eye. Once you are confident of your aim take a moment to breath and after you fully exhale simply release the arrow and string."

Slowly inhaling and then right as she exhaled she released the string. The arrow shot off the bow and struck the target slightly left of where she was aiming.

He must have heard the arrow strike the mound of dirt because he told her, "Good job."

Turning her head slightly towards him she said, "Thank you."

She was looking directly at him. He was smiling broadly and she had to admit she found him very pleasant to be around. His arms were still around her and it made her feel safe.

Releasing his grasp around her he stated, "Get the arrow and try again."

"Alright." She said with a nod.

Jogging over to the mound she pulled the arrow out of the dirt. It was a little bit of a struggle but she got the arrow free. She ran back over to where she was standing.

"This time do it alone." He instructed her.

She set the arrow on the bow and then pulled back and aimed. Taking a long deep breath she once again fired once she finished exhaling. The arrow leapt off the bow and struck the spot that she was aiming. Giving out a little cheer of joy she grinned widely.

"I take it that you hit where you were aiming."

"Yes."

"Repeat it again."

Once again she collected the arrow and repeated the process. She hit the spot perfectly again.

After having her do it several times Proetus announced, "You are ready. Let us go back and collect my chiton then we will hunt down our dinner."

"Alright."

Medusa took his hand and guided him back to the cave. She let go of his hand once they were there and grabbed his chiton. It was still a little damp but it was more than dry enough to wear. She waved it in the air for a moment to dry it a little more. As she passed it back to him he immediately removed the blanket around his waist, leaving him naked.

She finally could not take it anymore so she asked, "Can I ask you something?"

"Sure." He replied as he slipped his chiton around himself.

Flushing in embarrassment from the question she finally spit it out, "Are all Argives so willing to bare themselves in front of others?"

Proetus laughed heartily for some time before finally stating, "If there was any doubt you are Athenian you have ended it."

Frowning at him she huffily stated, "Why do you think that?"

"Athenians are renown for their unnecessary modesty."

He grasped out with his hand, clearly a gesture for her to hold his hand. She took his hand.

"I am merely making a joke. No, normally we are not so willing to bare ourselves in front of others. In my current predicament I have little choice but to do what I need to do. I rely on you and in our few days of knowing each other I find myself completely trusting you. If my trust is making you uncomfortable I sincerely apologize."

A bit of guilt washed over her. Proetus was right. Being blind meant that many things a normal person could do for themselves he could no longer do. No doubt a normal man would not have fallen like he did earlier. He was completely reliant on her.

What she could only describe as a very jovial look crossed his face before he stated in what she could tell was a joking manner, "I hope at least you are enjoying what you see."

She did not know what propelled her to do it but she replied, “I am.”

CHAPTER 19

Instant regret hit Medusa as she realized what she had done. Proetus responded simply by laughing heartily.

After he finished laughing he must have decided to spare her more embarrassment because he just said, "Let us head off. I am hoping to have a successful hunt."

Sighing out in relief she took his hand and began to guide him towards the border between the forest and the farms. It was always the best spot to find hare. At least that is where she had always seen them during her many trips back and forth. The sun was now fully out and she was able to guide Proetus much easier through the forest.

As they got closer to the edge of the forest she let go of his hand and stated, "This is usually where I have seen the hare when I am out."

Proetus whispered, "Prepare your bow and wait."

Medusa prepared the bow and set an arrow into the string while being ready to pull the string. She made sure to sit as still as possible and breathe quietly. After standing there for some time she heard some rustling near a bush off to her right. Proetus gestured quietly with his hand at her. As she glanced at him he pointed towards the bush and then pulled his other hand as a hint she needed to pull the string on the bow. Turning towards the bush she pulled her string back and started to take aim. She breathed slowly and evenly while waiting to see the hare shuffling around. Finally it hopped into view and was nibbling on some of the leaves from the bush. Medusa took steady as aim as she could at the hare and after she exhaled she let go of the string. Her arrow launched off at the hare but instead of striking it, the arrow flew slightly over its head and landed into the ground. The hare ran off as fast as it could, disappearing out of sight.

Proetus softly asked, "You missed?"

Frowning heavily she said in a very disappointed tone, "Yes."

In what she guessed was a reassuring tone he told her, "It can be challenging. We will keep trying until you get one."

"Okay."

Proetus announced, "Let us move to another spot and wait."

Medusa collected the arrow that she shot into the bush and then took Proetus' hand to walk with him along the edge of the forest. She spotted a shrub with several berries and realized it might be a good choice for a possible target. Letting go of his hand she prepared to fire the bow. Time went by and she was starting to get tired of waiting. Right as she was about to move somewhere else she saw some movement in the bush. After a slight bit of wait with baited breath she spotted another hare. Trying to move as slow and careful as possible she aimed her bow at the hare. Evenly as she could while trying not to make noise she pulled back the arrow. After inhaling and exhaling slowly she released the arrow. It struck true and hit the hare right in its mid-section. It started to run and after going a slight distance it collapsed. Medusa let out a light cheer.

"You must have hit it."

"Yes."

"Let us go collect your prize."

"Okay." She said as she took his right hand.

They walked over to the hare and Medusa frowned. It was still alive and breathing very slow and unevenly.

"It is still alive." Medusa stated solemnly.

Proetus knelt down near it and grasped out before taking a hold of the hare's shoulders. He suddenly pulled out the sword Medusa had and in a brisk motion lopped off the hare's head. It was initially upsetting, especially since she did not see where he got her sword from. He was much more capable than she gave him credit for, especially with his blindness. Before she could say anything he pulled out the arrow, which was damaged from being imbedded in the creature, and then tossed it aside.

Next he grabbed the hare by its feet and declared, "Let us go find another one."

She felt more than a little guilty about killing the hare and was quite surprised by Proetus' heartlessness over it. Once he stood up she took his hand.

They walked along quietly for some time before Proetus asked, "Are you okay?"

"Yes why?" She responded.

"You are barely holding my hand whereas before you would clasp it tightly when we walked."

"Oh sorry." She responded before holding his hand firmly.

He then declared, "You can be honest with me Medusa."

Finally she just told him, "I felt bad about killing it."

Proetus stopped walking and as he grasped her hand he pulled her closer towards him.

He set his hand tenderly on her cheek before saying, "You really are a kind soul. In our situation we cannot afford tenderness when we need to eat."

"I understand."

"Will you be able to continue?"

"It was just a shock initially."

"Alright. Shall we go try again and then we will take a break for a day?"

"Yes."

Stepping away from him she again took his hand to guide him along the edge of the forest. They were successful and killed two more hare before heading back to the cave. It was well past lunch time and she was very hungry. Proetus guided her on how to gut and skin it. She used some of it to make stew with several vegetables and she had to admit that it was delicious.

Proetus declared, "It is wonderful. Worth the hunt."

"Yes it was."

His face shifted to a more serious look before he said, "I needed to talk with you about something."

Nerves immediately ran through her.

Cautiously she responded, "Which is?"

"Well," He replied before rubbing his chin and then continuing, "I had initially planned to head off to Sami to look for work or some other thing since I know I can never return home. I have found myself with a sudden change of heart."

Trying to find out where he was headed with this conversation she asked, "How so?"

"I find myself wanting to stay here with you."

Joy hit her initially but then she remembered that she was cursed as a hideous monster. Sooner or later Proetus would find out and seeing him flee in panic was probably the best possible result. She imagined that he could even try to attack her if he found out what she had become.

"Medusa?"

Proetus saying her name interrupted her thoughts so she answered, "Yes."

"What do you think?" He asked.

She swore that he actually sounded nervous. Maybe he was as attracted to her as she was him?

Being honest she told him, "I would like that."

A wide grin crossed his face as he stated, "Of course I will try my best to not weigh you down by helping any way that I can."

"You have not been a burden."

Proetus laughed heartily before saying. "You are too kind. From dragging me all over the place, feeding me constantly, and having to embarrass yourself by dragging me out of a pond bare naked there is no doubt I have been a burden."

Feeling a bit more comfortable about being around him she stated, "The last one was not a burden."

Proetus laughed uproariously before declaring, "Maybe you are not such a shy Athenian. Since it is just us alone I am going to confess that I am hoping to repeat it in the near future."

Medusa's heart skipped with joy. He was just as attracted to her as she was him. Maybe it was being alone for the last few years but she found herself much bolder than she used to be. She set down her plate and moved over to him. Kneeling down so she was looking right into his eyes. Leaning forward she kissed him on the lips. He responded to her kiss by grabbing her shoulders and kissing back. Proetus pulled her closer towards him and began to wrap his arms around her shoulders and back. She was being overwhelmed by the passion of the moment but realized that she had to tell him the truth.

Pulling away from him she said, "I need to tell you the truth."

She slid slightly away from him.

"The truth?" He asked with a confused look on his face.

"I am from Piraeus like I said but my family never died."

"Oh. What happened?"

Giving a heavy sigh Medusa told him everything. From the day she left Piraeus for Athens and up to when she met him. She explained what happened at the Parthenon and how she was cursed. His facial expression went from complacent to confused and finally to what she guessed was upset.

"I do not believe you are the monster you claim to be. I held you in my arms and felt your bare skin against me. You are so kind and caring. Something a monster is not."

Looking down at the ground she told him, "It is true. Athena cursed me for something that was not my fault."

"I do not believe it." He stated resolutely.

"Well you cannot see me so my curse seems to not affect you but it is true."

"Let me feel." He commanded.

She was highly hesitant to let him feel the hideous snakes on her head.

Proetus restated in a firm tone, "Let me feel."

"I fear if I do you will leave me." She solemnly told him.

Part of her wished that she had just lied to him. Surely she could have kept the secret from him for a long time? Maybe even forever? Now that he knew it meant that what she thought was going to be a possible relationship was now completely over with.

"Medusa?"

"Fine. If you wish to leave afterwards I will understand."

She moved back over to him and then unwrapped the himation she had around her head. Once in front of him she placed his hands on her cheeks. His hands slowly moved up her face until they made contact with her temples. He stopped for a brief moment. The expression on his face was confusion. Slowly he moved his hands up until they finally made contact with the base of one of the snakes that now made up her hair. He rapidly pulled his hands away as his facial expression shifted to panic. Medusa scurried away from him before he could lash out.

There was a long silence before he finally said, "It is true."

Glancing downward in shame she whispered out, "Yes."

She could not tell if the look on his face was one of disappointment or fear. He was clearly quite upset. He suddenly stood up. She shuffled away a bit just in case he lashed out.

"I need to go." He said before slowly walking away.

Turning to watch him walk away she wanted to go after him but she knew that he did not wish her to. Tears began to well up in her eyes as she realized that it was probably the last time that she would see him. His arms moved about from side to side as he dodged a tree before continuing out of sight. Once he was gone she flung herself to the ground and sobbed uncontrollably. She was a damned fool to think that he would stay once he knew what she really was. After lying there crying to herself for a while she pulled herself off of the ground. She heard several of her chicken clucking as they scraped the ground. Medusa sprinkled a few bits of grain before opening the pen and taking a seat. Anthousa strutted up to her.

Picking up the hen Medusa stated, "You still love me, even though I am hideous."

She gave the hen a light hug and she ran her fingers over Anthousa's head. Anthousa clucked lightly before hopping back down on the ground to pick at a piece of grain. Medusa stood up and then stepped out of the pen. Sadness overwhelmed her even though she had to know that the reality was no one would want anything to do with a monster like her. The idea that she might have to move to another spot crossed her mind. If Proetus decided to tell others about her she would be in danger. First thing in the morning she would search out another spot. It would have to be very far away from where she was but close enough to the coast that she could still get fish. She sighed heavily as she thought about how much work it was going to be to move all of her things. It was something that she had to do but she was not looking forward to doing it. The sun had started to set so she decided to go to sleep. Tomorrow was going to be a very long day. After taking off her sandals she slid onto her bed and stared up into the ceiling of the cave. Thinking about Proetus made her very sad. Her childish dreams had turned into a nightmare. Closing her eyes she finally fell off to sleep.

* * * * *

"Medusa?" A male voice called out waking her from her sleep.

In a hurry she sat up. It took her a moment to recognize that the voice was that of Proetus. At first she was hit with a sense of hope but then the idea that he could be here to hurt her crossed her mind. Moving as quickly as she could she got out of her bed and then slid on her sandals. Stepping out into the dark she cautiously looked around.

"Medusa?" Proetus called out once again.

He was barely visible but she spotted him tapping a branch wildly as a way to navigate through the forest. She kept quiet to make sure that he was alone. She could not see or hear anyone else. After he continued to wander for a bit she decided that he was alone.

Stepping carefully as possible she walked close enough that he would be able to hear her before she whispered, "Proetus?"

He stopped walking and then turned towards her. Next using the stick in his hand he guided himself towards her.

As he got only a little bit away from her he said, "I wandered the forest lost for some time thinking about everything. For the longest time my life was laid out in front of me with a clear path. A life of luxury was my fate. All it took was one incident to completely ruin my entire life before leaving me broken and alone."

It was then that she realized they were the same. Until that cruel goddess ruined Medusa's life she was headed to become the wife of a very wealthy man and live a life of luxury. It probably was not going to be as opulent as to what Proetus was headed towards but she was going to have servants who would pamper her every need. She said nothing to him.

He continued, "You too were ruined by one incident as well."

Softly she responded, "Yes."

"I need to know something."

"What is that?" She asked him.

Pausing for a moment he finally asked, "Why did you stop to help me?"

The question was confusing so she asked, "What do you mean?"

"When I was wandering lost. Why did you stop to help me?"

Medusa answered, "Because you needed help."

Stepping even closer, he reached out with his hand to feel for her. She took his hand.

"I cannot see how people respond to me when I am around others but I can hear it in their voices. A mixture of disgust and fear. My face is hideously scarred and without my sight I am a burden to others. I imagine people react the same to you."

She did not know why she said it but with a chuckle she replied, "Only for a brief moment before they turn to stone."

He tugged on her arm and pulled her closer so that she was pressed into him before stating, "It is a good thing that I am blind then I guess."

Leaning forward he kissed her on the tip of her nose. Medusa chuckled because she realized that he missed his target. He shifted his lips down and started to kiss her on the lips.

CHAPTER 20

Medusa stirred awake. The first thing that she saw Proetus' bare chest that she was lying on. One of her blankets was covering them as they lay naked on her bed. Her himation was still wrapped around her head, which was good because the last thing that she wanted was one of those snakes biting him. His left arm was draped around her and resting on her back. It was so warm and comfortable that she did not want to move. Proetus' slow and even breathing was the only sound that she could hear. Off by the entrance of her cave she could see light peeking in. Pretty soon Georgios was going to make all sorts of noise to get his breakfast. As if on cue Georgios began squawking loudly.

Proetus stirred for a moment before he spoke, "Good morning."

"Good morning to you too."

She felt his hand that was sitting on her back slowly moving.

"Your skin is so soft."

"Thank you. I do not get to treat it with olive oil very often but when I can I do."

"Where do you get olives from? I think it would take much longer to grow your own tree."

She blushed before admitting, "I help myself to olives from the trees in the farms."

"Ahhh."

"I did plant one but it does take forever to grow."

Giving a chuckle he commented, "Well we have to do what we have to do sometimes."

"Speaking of which I am going to have to expand the garden today."

"Do you need any help?" He asked.

"I will take care of it."

"Alright."

Remembering that she wanted to make some more blankets and a chiton for him she told him, "Later today I am going to have to leave you here so I can collect some wool."

"What do you need wool for?"

"I am going to make you another chiton. The one you have is very old."

Proetus laughed heartily before stating, "You are already taking care of me."

"You came back even though I am a monster."

"No," He stated firmly before continuing, "You are no monster."

Picking up her head she gave him a kiss.

When she broke their kiss he told her, "The garden can wait."

Wrapping both of his arms around her once again, he pulled her all the way on top of him.

* * * * *

After getting dressed and feeding her chicken Medusa made breakfast for her and Proetus. It was insane how quickly he had changed her life. He was so tender with her. Not since she was home with her father was any man kind to her. The fact they had so much in common only made things better to her. He was an outcast just like her. Glancing over at him she saw that he was eating his breakfast. She had made eggs but with meat from the hare in it. The last few days with him had really slowed down her collecting of supplies. She would have to work hard to catch up. It was not a big deal especially after making love with Proetus she was so happy that a little extra work meant nothing. After taking Proetus to the pond to bath, and more lovemaking, she brought him back to the cave and got to work. She had to extend each row out, probably about twice the size it was, and then maybe look at acquiring more chicken. When she first fled the Parthenon she felt bad about stealing but at this point she accepted it was part of her life.

"I am going to get started on the garden so sit back and relax." She told him.

"Alright." He replied as he set back in the chair he was sitting in.

Medusa picked up a stick and slowly dug out the garden. She was going to have to remove a bunch of weeds and a large bush in order to get it where she wanted it. It took her some serious work to get it finished but she was quite happy with the results. One of the best things about Kefalonia was the weather. During the winter it never got so cold that she could not work on her garden and during the summer the weather did not get real hot like Athens. It took all of her seeds to fill the garden and she had to run back and forth to the pond a few times until she was done. It was a bit past lunch time so after cleaning her hands she made something for them to eat.

As they sat there eating Proetus asked, "I was thinking if it would be possible for you to get me that lyre you mentioned that you had?"

"What do you need it for?"

"It has been a long while but I used to play one and I thought it would be a nice way to entertain myself while you go collect wool."

"Of course. I did not know you could play."

He stated, "It has been a long time but since I have nothing else to do with my time…"

Medusa chuckled at him before asking, "What other talents do you have?"

With a coy look on his face he replied, "You have already learned about some of them."

Medusa laughed as a response to his joke.

"Let me get you that lyre." She replied before strolling into the cave and picking up her lyre.

As she placed it into his hands he began playing with the strings. Next she collected a large blanket to hold the wool that she was going to borrow, the sword to sheer it, and a bag to carry some olives.

"I am going to collect some wool and some olives. Do you need anything before I go?"

"A kiss."

She grinned widely before leaning forward and giving him a kiss on the lips. His hand clasped her left arm as he kissed her back.

Breaking her kiss she stated, "I will be back as soon as I can."

"Please be careful out there."

"I will." She replied as she started walking away.

"Medusa?"

Turning around she answered, "Yes?"

"I love you."

It was quite a surprise to hear him say it. She was also very joyful to hear it.

"I love you too." She told him.

A massive grin was plastered on her face as she strolled away. She was able to find enough wool to make a chiton and an extra blanket plus plenty of olives to maybe at least moisturize her face. After getting back to her cave she made dinner before heading off to bed with Proetus.

* * * * *

It had been more than a few weeks since Proetus returned and Medusa could not have found herself any happier. The new extended garden was starting to grow, she had made him a new chiton, and after adding seven new hens to the group she had Proetus help her extend the pen. Today she was going to help Proetus practice using his stick to walk around. They had spent the last two weeks having him learn where everything was around them and it had worked great. Proetus was able to navigate from everything around the cave and up to the pond. She was impressed with how quickly he adapted, it was not long until he was helping her in the garden. Once they finished practicing his ability to learn where they where she brought him back to the cave for lunch. She made broiled hare for lunch. Since Proetus taught her how to hunt with a bow they had a plentiful supply of meat. After lunch she laid out a blanket out in front of the cave and they laid there snuggling. Whenever she was close to him she made sure to keep a himation tightly wrapped around her head.

"Medusa?"

"Yes?"

"I know you are probably uncomfortable about talking about it but I was curious about your… condition."

She let out a deep sigh before saying, "Whenever someone looks into my eyes they turn to stone statues. Not their clothing just their flesh. All of my beautiful blonde hair fell out and these hideous snakes grew in their place. Lastly my skin turned a light greenish yellow color."

"Have the snakes ever bit you?"

"No. Although they seem to respond to my mood sometimes. If I am upset they get agitated. If I am calm or happy they are relaxed. I do not know if they are dangerous to others so I keep them wrapped up when I am close to you."

Giving a chuckle he commented, "I appreciate that."

They laid there for some time with his hand slowly running up and down her left arm before Proetus told her, "I have heard tales of creatures that were described like you."

"How so?"

"Well, the stories I heard were that they were born of the gods and worked together as servants of Athena. I had not really thought much about the stories but from what you describe they were like you. Anything else of note you can think of?"

She thought about it for a moment before answering, "I have looked at myself in a reflection of water and it had no effect on me. Animals seem unaffected completely. Other than that I can think of nothing."

Chuckling Proetus stated, "Well I think that any of your kind would be immune to the effect."

"That makes sense."

"Yes it does. I believe that they were immortal in the stories I heard and that they had a hatred of all men."

Giving a little chuckle Medusa stated, "I do not hate men."

Proetus laughed uproariously before he declared, "I have noticed."

Medusa sat up and then climbed onto Proetus' lap while he was lying down.

Reaching out with her right hand she softly stroked his cheek before saying, "Thank you for coming back. I could die now and it would be happy."

Proetus lifted his arm up as though he was reaching for her. She took his hand and placed it on her cheek.

Once his hand was on her face he said, "I cannot imagine being happier anywhere else. I just hope you are not immortal as I would hate for you to suffer alone."

"I do not think I am immortal. I arrived on Kefalonia a girl."

Proetus slowly brought his hand off her cheek, down her shoulder, and then rested it on her hip.

"You are no girl."

Medusa laughed before grinding her hips into his lap and stating, "No, I am not."

A loud rustling noise came from off on her right away from the cave. Spinning her head she looked over at the bush.

Proetus asked, "What was that?"

She nervously watched the bushes while placing her hands on her himation in case she needed to remove it. After a few moments the bushes rustled again before a large beast stepped out. Medusa immediately recognized it as one of the ones who had chased her some time ago. This one was a bit bigger than that one was. Since then she had found out that they were called boars.

"It is a boar." She stated.

"How big?" Proetus asked calmly.

She was utterly surprised by how calm he seemed to be about this. She was in a panic and ready to run, although there was nowhere to go. If she ran into the cave she would be trapped.

"Very." She finally got out.

Proetus shifted underneath her before gently sliding her over and standing up.

He turned to her and asked, "Is this the first time it is here?"

"Yes. I have seen others but it was by the farms not here."

"Then it is wandering lost. Hand me the sword please."

Giving a nod Medusa stepped backwards slowly and walked towards the cave. Bending down she scooped up the sword and then walked back to Proetus. She handed him the sword. Suddenly out of nowhere Proetus raised the sword and yelled out loudly while swinging it wildly. The boar jumped and snuffled while clearly looking at Proetus in fear. Yelling out even louder Proetus jumped towards the boar. It responded by turning and running in fear. She heard it crash and smash loudly through the underbrush. After a moment the sound of it running got quieter and quieter until the forest was silent.

Proetus turned back around towards her and chuckled before declaring, "Wild animals will almost always run if the option is available when something bigger charges them."

"That makes sense. I know I always try to run when something bigger charges me." Medusa stated in a humorous tone.

He laughed at her joke. She took the sword from him and then guided him back to the blanket. As he moved to lay back down she set the sword up against the entrance of the cave and then spun back around to go lie with him. With all of her chores caught up she was quite happy with her use of free time. As she settled back down next to him her stomach suddenly rocked in nausea. She had been feeling ill on and off occasionally for a few days but did not think much of it.

He must have noticed it because he asked, "Are you well?"

"Yes, thank you. The last few days my stomach has been upset every once in a while."

"Did you eat something I did not? I have felt fine."

Taking a moment to think she could not think of anything. She was the one who cooked everything and she was confident that she did so exactly how her mother had taught her. There was nothing that she ate that he did not.

"No." She finally answered him.

"Very unusual."

"Yes it…" She started to speak before her stomach roiled violently and she was forced to shift over to her side and vomit.

Her throat burned from vomiting.

"Medusa? Are you well?" Proetus asked nervously.

She used the loose end of her himation to wipe her mouth. Her stomach felt a little better but she was still a bit nauseous.

Finally she answered, "Sorry I vomited."

"Do you feel better?"

"Yes but I still am feeling queasy."

"Ahhh. Do you have a fever? Sore muscles?"

"No," She responded.

"Hrmmm…" He replied thoughtfully before finally asking, "Can I ask you something personal?"

Medusa laughed. They were lovers. She saw no reason that he could not ask her anything.

"Of course." She firmly told him.

"When was the last time you bled?"

"Bled?" She asked very confused by his line of questioning.

"Yes. How women tend to do every few weeks."

"Oh…" She replied sullenly.

She had not thought about that. It had been many weeks since she last had menstruated. Just then it dawned on what was going on. Making love with Proetus several times every day had caused her to become pregnant.

CHAPTER 21

"I…" She stammered out before continuing, "I think I am pregnant."

Proetus' face shifted to a very stunned look.

After a very long pause he asked, "Is that even possible?"

Medusa frowned. Thoughts of all of the problems that this was going to cause ran through her head. Even though Proetus said that people like her would be immune to her curse she did not wish to pass it on to any children. It was a horrible thing to place on anyone, especially a child.

Before she could say anything else he stated, "I guess it is."

"Yes." She solemnly said.

"What is wrong?" Proetus asked with a concerned tone.

"I am worried about bringing a child into the world to be cursed as I am."

He rubbed his chin before declaring, "I am not sure that is how it works.

"What do you mean?"

"I do not think that curses are shared with a family member."

She frowned. If their child was born normal then it would just be turned to stone as any normal person would be by looking into her eyes?

"But I would end up harming them by looking into their eyes."

Proetus paused without saying a word. His face appeared to be conflicted. She guessed that he must have realized that what she stated was true. Assuming that her curse would not transfer to her children then they would simply be turned to stone once they glanced at her. Giving out a heavy sigh she slumped back down onto the blanket lying next to Proetus. He reached out with his hand and wrapped his arm around her before he started to softly run his fingers along her arm.

After a very long moment of silence he asked, "How did you keep from turning everyone around you when you go to the village to stone?"

"I wrap a himation around my head and keep my face in shadow so they cannot see my face." Medusa stated.

"Hrmm… Maybe that is what you will have to do with our child."

"I could slip or they could slip. Then I will end up ruining them."

"What else can we do?" He asked.

"I do not know."

"Medusa, do you not see what this is?"

She was confused by his question so she asked, "What do you mean?"

"It is a gift from the gods."

Medusa left out a harsh and very loud laugh before declaring, "The gods? They have no kindness. They have no mercy. They are clearly selfish and petty beings."

"And yet somehow I came into your life and now you bear my child?"

She froze. Proetus was right that while Athena ruined everything in her life with that evil curse Medusa was now in a place where she was quite happy. Being around Proetus and acting as his wife, although they were technically not married, had brought her significant joy. Tenderly she placed both of her hands on her stomach. It felt perfectly normal. Over the last few years of living in this cave she had lost every single bit of excess body fat that she had from her comfortable life in Piraeus. Her stomach was perfectly flat and her body was all lean muscle. She chuckled to herself thinking how her body was about to go through a lot.

"What are you laughing about?" Proetus asked her.

"I was just thinking how this baby is going to ruin my body."

Proetus laughed robustly before finally stating, "A price well worth paying to bring a life into the world."

"Easy for you to say since I will be the one paying it."

He took her hand before saying, "I will be here the whole time."

Turning her head to look over at him she grinned. She knew that it was going to be a struggle but she saw no reason why they could not at least try. After all the gods must have brought Proetus into her life for a reason. Leaning forward she kissed the back of his hand that was holding hers. It was the best that she could hope for. Maybe things would work out and they would have a beautiful child together. The next thought was what she would do in order to have this baby and raise it. The idea of a blindfold came into her mind. She could use it to cover her child's eyes.

Proetus stunned her out of her thoughts when he asked, "What are you thinking about?"

"I was trying to come up with different things that I could do to protect our child from my curse."

"There is a good chance they might even be immune to it from being your child."

"You think so?"

He shrugged his shoulders as he replied, "I do not see why not but who knows what will happen until it happens. We can only do the best we can."

Giving out a long drawn-out sigh she replied, "I suppose. I am just so worried. There is nothing I would love more than to be a mother but I dread the idea that I could accidentally harm my own child because of this damned curse."

"I know."

"Okay."

Medusa softly rubbed her hands on her stomach. It was so hard to imagine the life that was growing in there. Truly if anything was a gift from the gods it was the life that they gave to their people. She looked up into the sky. It was now deep into the winter season on Kefalonia. The weather was a bit colder but it was still very pleasant. She was quite grateful to the fact that the weather on the whole island was much cooler than Athens. She had to make an extra himation for Proetus to wrap around his shoulders for the cooler days. Leaning her head onto his shoulder she grinned. Starting tomorrow she was going to start collecting wool from sheep outside her normal area to start making clothing for the baby. Making woolen clothing was a bit of work but it was the sturdiest clothing that she could make. As she looked skyward she noted that the sun was starting to set. It was time to make dinner and then probably get some sleep. Slowly she pried herself off of the ground and cooked dinner. Tomorrow was going to be a busy day to start getting ready for this baby. After making dinner for the both of them they headed off to bed. She faded off to sleep quickly while cuddling against Proetus' bare skin.

* * * * *

Georgios' loud squawking woke her up the next morning. She sat up.

Proetus stating, "That silly bird loves to wake us up every morning just to get his damned grain."

Medusa laughed heartily before replying, "He has always been demanding. Let me go feed them and then I will cook our breakfast. Will it be okay for me to go and collect some wool?"

"Of course. What are you going to make?"

"I am going to make some baby clothes and a small blanket for them."

He chuckled before saying, "You are excited about the baby already?"

She nodded before telling him, "As a child I have always wanted my own baby and now that I have one coming I cannot wait until I am holding him or her."

"I feel the same way. If I am honest I am praying for a boy. I have always wanted to have a son to teach the Argive ways. It has been the greatest honor to serve Argos and hopefully someday our son will be able to go to Argos and serve its people."

"I would hope that he is not cursed like me so that he could do those things."

Proetus grinned at her before declaring, "Have faith. Sure the gods can be cruel but everything serves a purpose."

"I guess. Let us get started, I have a long ways to go in order to get to a new location for wool."

"Why the change?"

"If I keep taking from the same sheep the owners will notice so I like to go to different ones in order to avoid that."

"Ahhh, that makes sense."

Medusa stood up and strolled out to feed the chicken. They reacted with excitement when she came out. Scooping up the bucket she sprinkled a bit of grain. Her bucket was getting low again so tomorrow she would have to borrow more grain. She quickly whipped up a breakfast with some strips of meat from their most recent hunt. Over the last few weeks she had become quite good at shooting her bow. She also got very good at making arrows. Proetus had taught her well. It made her realize that even blinded he would probably do a wonderful job of being a father to a son, if they had one. Of course if they had a daughter it was going to be up to Medusa to teach her everything that she would need to know to be a fine wife. She had no idea how they would coordinate any sort of match. Maybe Proetus could do so. It would be something that they would worry about once their child was born. Once they finished eating Medusa gave Proetus a goodbye kiss before grabbing a blanket, her knife and the bag that she would need. She headed off towards the north. Normally she would head towards the rising sun to find sheep but today she decided to head north. She had not been there for a long time. The last time she was there she found a large valley that was surrounded by the same mountains in which her cave was set in. In that valley she knew that there were many sheep wandering about that she could not count them. She very rarely ever went there because the terrain was so rough. It was going to take a bit of time to go there but since she wanted to find new pastures to borrow from she had to do what she had to do. Reaching down, she patted on her stomach.

"I hope I can give you everything you want." She told her growing baby.

She sighed because basic survival was the best that she could do. Suddenly she was hit with the inspiration to find a book if possible. She imagined that they were quite rare but maybe in Sami there would be one. As a grown woman she doubted that she would be under the same assault as she was dressed as a dirty beggar. It would be something to look for in the next few days. Whether she had a boy or a girl, it was going to be important that they know how to read and write. Only the poorest of people could do neither and she wanted to find a way to help her child. Maybe she could look into finding more silver to collect that way when her child was ready to go out on their own they could do so more easily. Her mind had wandered a lot since the discovery of her pregnancy. Her stomach still roiled from sickness. If it was just a normal sickness she should have recovered by now. There could be no doubt in her mind that she was with child.

Smiling happily she said, "Thank Artemis for my child."

Right then she arrived at the point where the forest broke into the secluded field. There was three massive herds of sheep. Taking a moment to examine them she spotted the largest herd was only being watched by a single shepherd. It was going to be her best bet for stealing some wool. Medusa slipped her himation over herself in order to cover her head. It would have been wrong to turn some innocent person into stone for something so silly as wool. She crept along the edge of the open plain near the forest so she could sneak up to the herd. Once she got close enough but was still out of sight she cut off as much wool as she could from random sheep. Generally she liked to target the bellies so maybe when a harvest was done the owners might not notice. It took her almost half a day but finally she had enough to head back home. While walking back home she whistled joyfully. Proetus was waiting for her when she arrived back in the cave. Part of her wondered how he did not go insane sitting around so much. She knew that he did practice with her old sword but that had to get boring.

"You are back." He announced when she approached.

For some reason she swore that his hearing was getting sharper.

Shrugging it off she responded, "Yes, I got plenty of wool."

"That is good. Listen, I wanted to make sure to let you know that I am thankful to have you in my life. You are an amazing woman."

Flushing at him all she could say in response was, "Thank you. You are amazing as well."

After dinner they headed off to bed. Tomorrow was going to be a long day of working with all of this wool.

CHAPTER 22

Medusa grinned while holding Proetus' hand. They were heading to Sami in order to find a book. She had already finished making everything else that her baby would need, which took a bit over a month. Her once flat stomach was now a small expanding bump. It brought her great joy when it started because it was a confirmation of her pregnancy. Even while just walking along, her free hand kept finding itself resting on her stomach. Proetus seemed just as excited as she was. In their current conditions they had found happiness together. It was the closest thing to a normal life either could have. She was joyful for it.

As they got closer she whispered, "We are almost there."

"Alright. I am certain with me here you should not have any issues from uncouth people."

"What if we do?"

Proetus laughed before answering, "They will find themselves very surprised by the abilities of a blind man."

She nodded at him. As they approached the village she made sure that her himation was in place and fully covering her face. The last thing that they needed was someone finding out about her curse in this town. The town looked exactly the same. She spotted Athena's temple off to her right. There was more buildings along the outskirts. They looked newer but were still made from crude dried mud blocks. She forgot how simple the town was in comparison to Athens. It had been years since she had last been here. There was a nice market in the middle of the town so she guided Proetus there. Many of the people there gave her an odd look but she guessed having Proetus there kept them from saying anything.

Medusa approached one of the booths and asked the elderly woman wearing an old dingy chiton, "Do you know if anyone has a book for sale?"

She laughed before stating, "No but good luck."

Proetus interrupted by asking, "Why do you say good luck?"

"Not too many folks here read."

Grumpily Medusa added, "We shall see."

"Indeed. I wish you luck." The elderly woman retorted with a chuckle.

Pulling on Proetus' arm she headed towards the next booth. Bouncing from booth to booth she finally found a man selling a book. The man, who she guessed was only a little older than she was, gave her the impression that he had stolen the book. He was wearing a heavily stained chiton, a pair of leather sandals, and a very thin beat-up looking wrap around his shoulders. He had a patchy beard and scraggly black hair. The man asked her for a drachma for the book. Taking a moment to examine the book she realized immediately that it was a retelling of how the gods came into being. Not an ideal topic as she was not a fan of the gods but it would allow her child to learn to read. She bought the book and put it into her bag.

Turning to the man she asked, "Is there a temple for Artemis nearby?"

"There is a shrine just outside Sami that way." He answered while pointing away from where she came from.

"Thank you."

"Of course."

She guided Proetus away from the man and down the direction the man had pointed. It was in the opposite direction of the way she had entered the town.

With curiosity in his voice Proetus asked, "Why are we headed to Artemis' shrine? Are you planning to pray to her?"

"I am not going to pray to her but I made some extra clothing for babies to offer for protection of our child."

"Wise. It is best to honor the gods, even when we do not want to."

She grunted at his words. Medusa was not enthused about honoring gods, especially Athena or Poseidon, but she felt that she had to do anything and everything for her child. Even if it meant swallowing a little bit of her pride. As they walked out of the town she spotted the shrine. It was a simple small altar with a wooden crate sitting next to the altar. Hovering over the altar was a marble statue of Artemis. She was posed in an epic stance with her bow pulled back as though she was shooting at a nearby wild animal. On her back was a quiver and resting on her short hair was a laurel of some kind. Medusa guided Proetus to the front of the altar and then helped him to kneel. She knelt down next to the altar and paused silently for a moment. Honestly she had no idea what she was supposed to do. After a bit of a wait she rose from her feet and then she helped Proetus stand. Stepping over to the crate she took a look at it. The crate was empty but she guessed that the idea of the crate was to set any offerings inside it. Reaching into her bag she pulled out everything that she had made. It was several small woolen blankets and a few wraps for a baby's diaper.

"Ready?" He asked her.

"Yes. Let us go home."

He pulled on her arm to get her closer before giving her a hug. She gave him a light kiss on the lips before they headed off. It was a quite pleasant walk back to the cave. Since the sun was starting to set she took the opportunity to stop and pick a few handful of olives on their way home. Once they got home she made dinner. Proetus had made some torches so she took the opportunity to set one up outside the front of the cave so she could read from the book. It was old and pretty beat up but she felt that it would more than work.

"Read it to me." Proetus instructed her.

She began to read from the first page. It talked about the titans and how Zeus was born. She read several pages before closing the book and putting it away. It was time to go to sleep. They went to bed and after once again making love she drifted off to sleep.

* * * * *

Something woke Medusa from her slumber as she sat up. It was still dark outside and Proetus was sleeping. She looked around and heard nothing. Her chicken were completely quiet. Carefully she slipped off of the bed to take a look outside. Peeking out the entrance of her cave she noticed that that sunset was barely starting. It was only a brief time before the Georgios was going to wake Proetus up with his loud noise. Picking up the bucket she sprinkled some grain out for them, which woke the sleeping birds. She had one day of grain left so today or tomorrow she was going to have to get more grain. Next, she stepped out into her garden and began to examine the plants. The new plants she had set up were growing very nicely with some fruit already beginning to come out. She scraped out a few weeds that were starting to sprout up. After checking her garden she decided to collect a few eggs and then prepare breakfast. She figured that Proetus would probably wake up soon. Usually if she fed Georgios before full sunrise he would keep quiet so Proetus would rise whenever he had enough sleep. Thankfully she had plenty of both hare and fish so she could pick either. She went with hare because she found it tasted better than fish to her. Maybe it was the fact the majority if her life included lots of fish in her meals but she really liked hare better.

"I see you are awake." A voice that she recognized immediately as Proetus said from near the entrance of the cave.

She turned to look at him. He was wearing his chiton and in his hand was the stick he used to guide himself around the cave.

"See?" She smarmily asked him.

Giving a hearty laugh Proetus replied, "Not literally of course."

"I know." Medusa replied with a light chuckle before continuing, "Have a seat. I am preparing breakfast."

"Alright. What are we going to be doing today?"

As she handed him the plate and guide him into sitting down she replied, "I… am going to collect some grain for the bucket. You are going to stay here and keep a close eye on Anthousa."

"Did she escape again?"

Shaking her head at him she replied, "No but she has found her way on the top of the pen so I am sure she wants to."

Once again Proetus chuckled.

He then commented, "You were not kidding when you said that she was a troublemaker."

Taking a seat next to him Medusa began to eat breakfast. Once they were done eating she gave him a kiss before heading off to the farms. It was the farms just before the fishing village where the most grain was grown. She wrapped her himation firmly around her head. It was then that she noticed something about herself she had not noticed before. The snakes on her head were longer! It was so gradual over the last few years that she had not noticed it but as she aged the snakes seemed to grow like her hair used to. Thinking hard about it she remembered when she first was cursed and saw her reflection the snakes were maybe two hand lengths. Now they were easily almost the length of her arm! Medusa grumbled to herself. She had been so happy with Proetus that she almost forgot about the snakes coming out of her head. Giving a sigh she shrugged while she continued to walk along. It took some time but she finally got to the farm where they were growing grain. Off in the distance she spotted dozens of workers harvesting grain. She pulled out the knife that she brought and ducked down to begin cutting off stalks. Slowly and evenly she filled her bucket while making sure to keep low. Once the bucket was full she slipped away and headed home. The walk home was easy and before long she was giving Proetus a slight kiss on the lips.

"I guess you had no issues?" He asked her.

"No concerns."

"What would you do if someone ever spotted you?"

She paused for a moment to think about it before finally answering, "I would run."

"And if you cannot run?"

"The times I have not run people ended up being turned to stone."

"Well… come sit down and read more to me?"

Giving a nod she answered, "I need to split the seeds from this grain and then I will read for you okay?"

"Of course."

Sitting down she dumped out the stalks of grain out on the ground and then slowly began to separate the grain from the stalk. She made sure to toss the stalks into the garden so they could decompose as she dropped the seeds of grain into the bucket. Once she finished with her task she placed the bucket back on a rock and out of reach of her chicken. The last thing that she would want is for the chicken to get a hold of the bucket. Dusting off her hands she got her book. She realized that due to its age she was going to have to store it high in order to keep her child from ruining it. As she sat down in her chair she opened the book and flipped to where she was last reading. This part of the book talked about how Zeus defeated the titans in order to gain power as the ruler of the gods. She had heard all of this before from her mother when she was a child.

Proetus interrupted, "This is my favorite story."

She was surprised about his declaration. The idea of the titans gobbling children whole seemed insane.

"How so?" She asked him.

"The willingness of Rhea to disobey her own husband in order to protect her child is inspiring. I do wonder how one could eat their own child whole but not notice after several children that the next one was just a big stone."

Medusa chuckled. Many times she heard these stories and they seemed nothing short of silly. Ironically her own fate and actually meeting two of the gods let her know that there must have been some truth to the stories. She wondered how much of them were true and how much was made up but there would never be a way for her to know for certain.

"Please continue." Proetus asked her.

She continued to read from the book for a while before deciding it was time to eat lunch. After lunch she asked Proetus to play his lyre. He had gotten so much better at playing it that she was starting to think he could have played for large audiences. After a bit of time he had convinced her to sing along with him.

She did not think that her voice was good but he seemed to greatly enjoy her singing. Honestly it was probably just because he loved her that he did not realize how bad her voice was. After tucking away the book she handed the lyre to Proetus and then sat down next to him.

"Sing along." He instructed her.

Medusa grumbled to herself. She did not want to sing. Looking over at him she saw his face was joyful as he began to play his lyre. She felt bad so she began to sing along. She sang along for a few songs before he stopped playing.

He turned to look at her as he said, "That was fun."

Suddenly a large bright glaring beam of like struck directly in front of them. Medusa covered her eyes to protect them. After a moment the brightness dimmed a good amount so she removed her hand from in front of her eyes and looked. She was stunned when she realized that now standing before her was the goddess Athena. Just like last time she was wearing a golden chiton and golden sandals. An owl was sitting on her shoulder.

"I had cursed you once before and I have not lifted my curse. You shall not know joy for defiling my temple."

"Who is that?" Proetus asked while turning his head towards Athena.

Athena gestured at Proteus before firmly declaring, "You are healed."

Frowning heavily Medusa turned to look at Proetus. His face glimmered over his eyes and after a few moments she could see the scars that once covered his face disappeared.

"My lesson will be learned." Athena bellowed before simply vanishing in air.

"I… I can see." Proetus declared while looking at her.

Panicking from realizing what Athena had done Medusa started to turn away from him so he could not look into her eyes. She moved too slowly and right as she tried to close her eyes he looked right into her eyes. Immediately he began to turn to stone. She bellowed out an angry scream.

CHAPTER 23

Medusa flung herself to the ground at the feet of the stone statue that was once Proetus. She cried uncontrollably. She just could not understand why Athena kept wanting to punish her. Medusa did nothing wrong in that damned temple and yet once again Athena struck out to ruin her life. It angered Medusa greatly. She had honestly thought that the gods had given back after taking so much only to have them take once again. Rolling onto her back staring upwards she saw Proetus, now all stone, looking over at her chair. As if to mock her even more, he appeared to have a smile on his face. It was almost as if he was happy to be able to look at her. Tears still spilled out of her eyes as she looked upwards. She had no idea what she could do now. Proetus had wrapped himself completely around her. On top of it all, she was still pregnant with his child. How could she possibly raise it alone? Most likely it would end up being a stone statue just like poor Proetus. As she lay there sobbing she finally realized that she had enough. From the moment she left her house in Piraeus she was abused and mistreated until she met Proetus. To have Athena take the one good thing from her life was more than enough for her.

"I will show you." Medusa angrily stated.

Standing up, which was a little more difficult than normal due to her being pregnant, she grabbed her himation and headed off. If Athena was going to strike against Medusa then Medusa was going to strike back. Walking as briskly as a pregnant woman could, she stomped along through the forest. Once she hit the edge of the border of the forest she wrapped her himation firmly around her head. The sun was not going to set for some time so she would have plenty of opportunity to strike her vengeance against Athena. As she approached Sami the sun was just starting to close in on the horizon. It was still plenty bright enough for her to see clearly but it would not be long until the sun fully set.

As she approached Sami one of the men who she guessed was a guard approached her and asked, “What brings you to Sami?”

She blew right by him as she replied, “I am here to visit the temple.”

The man said nothing as she continued walking directly towards the temple. As she walked along she spotted several people watching her. Noone said a word to her, which she believed was due to her recent visit. The temple itself came into full view as she approached. It was the only nearby building she saw that was made of marble. It was a much smaller looking version of the Parthenon in Athens. The biggest difference that she noticed as she got closer was the fact that the white marble seemed to actually not be the entire building. It was mostly made of wood and then a façade of marble placed in key spots. She grinned evilly. Her vengeance was going to be more complete than she thought it would be. A young woman wearing a thin white chiton and a white himation that was delicate set halfway on her head to hang off along her back approached Medusa.

The young woman spoke, “Can I help you today?”

Angrily Medusa stated, “Yes. You will be one of many to pay for Athena’s crimes against me.”

The woman’s facial expression shifted to confusion. Before she could react Medusa ripped off her himation and looked right at the woman. Her face shifted to fear before she suddenly turned to stone. Lashing out in anger with her left foot Medusa pushed the statue that was the woman onto the ground. She stepped into the temple and glanced around.

A loud scream echoed through the temple followed by a female voice yelling, “A monster!”

Right as she looked to see who it was she spotted several female priestesses looking at her in panic. Almost immediately as she looked at each one they turned to stone. Their facial expressions went from abject terror to disgust.

Strolling up to the first one Medusa screamed out, "Where is your precious Athena to protect you?"

Pushing out with her hand she knocked over the stone priestess. She knew it was wicked but why should she care? Athena kept pushing and pushing. So Medusa decided to push back. If Athena wanted her to be a monster, she decided that she will be the best monster that she could be. Along the back wall was a doorway leading either out of the temple or into another room. Boldly stepping through the door she was surprised to see that the room was an open area with several beds. It was likely where all of the priestesses slept. Three priestesses were cowering in the corner of the room and when Medusa entered they began begging.

"Look at me." Medusa ordered them.

They stopped crying and looked at her. Immediately all three turned into stone statues. Laughing loudly she felt so powerful. Athena turned her into a hideous monster and kept taking and taking so Medusa was taking back. This whole damned temple was going to pay for Medusa's pain. Stepping up to the three women, each of which had a slightly difference facial expression of terror, Medusa pushed on each one to knock them over. Spinning around she searched the back room to decide what to do next. There was an open fire in the middle of the room where the priestesses were probably cooking their dinner. A pot was hanging over it. A wicked thought hit her. She ripped off one of the cloth hangings from the wall and dragged it over to the fire. Turning these priestesses to stone was not enough. Medusa was going to burn this damned temple to the ground. Athena would feel this for certain. One thing Medusa knew from all the stories her mother told her was that the gods loved their adoration. The second she dragged the hanging over to the fire she pitched it in. Next she grabbed various bits of clothing and lined them up heading towards the woolen beds. She grabbed anything and everything that she could find which would start a fire and began tossing it towards the slowly growing fire. Once she was satisfied she spun on her heel and started to walk out.

"It is in the temple!" A male voice came from outside of the temple as Medusa entered the main area.

She grinned wickedly. More of Athena's precious worshipers were about to feel the wrath of Medusa's curse. Two very scared looking men entered with swords drawn. She took a step back behind the large statue of Athena set against the back wall.

"Are you scared?" She asked in a dark voice that echoed through the main temple room.

One of the men replied in a shaky voice, "Show yourself monster so we can end you."

Laughing heartily Medusa replied, "And yet your voice trembles in fear. I think if I stepped out of the shadows you both would scream in terror."

The same man spoke in a much more confident tone, "I doubt it monster."

Deciding to tease them more Medusa wrapped her himation around her head once again before stepping out. She made sure to pull her chiton tight to make it clear that she was pregnant.

"It is just a pregnant girl." The man stated.

She took a good look at both. They were just regular old villagers with swords. Both looked to be in their early twenties at best.

"I am. Tell me. Do either of you honor Athena?" She asked.

"Of course silly girl. Tell us where the monster is."

Rolling her head backwards she laughed loudly before calling out, "I am the monster!"

Flipping off her himation she exposed her face to the men. Their faces shifted in fear before both immediately turned to stone.

Giving a chuckle she sarcastically asked, "Who ended who?"

Strolling up to the first man she lashed out with a kick into his side. It tilted the statue of the man sideways and into the other statue. Both fell over and crashed into a nearby vase. A heavy smoke smell wafted to her nose from behind her. Turning back she saw that the wooden walls of the temple were catching fire. It worked better than she thought it would. She turned back around and as she strolled out of the temple shc wrapped her himation around her head. Off in the distance she heard a panic as many of the villagers scurried in response to the growing fire. She confidently walked away. Villagers holding buckets of water ran past her as she kept walking. She grinned evilly. They were in such a hurry that they did not seem to notice her. Once she was just outside of Sami she turned to watch the temple burn. It was burning out of control and she was confident that it could not be saved.

Speaking to no one in particular she stated angrily, "And if they rebuild it I will be back."

The sun had set a little more than halfway so she turned back around to head home. It was a long walk back through the farms and forest until she finally made it back to her cave. The sun had finally set so she started a fire in the dark and immediately she was once again hit with overwhelming grief. Proetus was now a stone statue sitting in one of her chairs. He was still holding the lyre in his hands and on his face was a smile. Reaching out she tenderly stroked his cheek. The first thought in her mind was how much she hated Athena. She wished that she could hurt that cruel goddess directly but what she did at Sami was probably the best that she would be able to do. Reaching out with her arms Medusa gave the statue of Proetus a hug. It was not the same and made her start crying all over again. Letting go of the statue she dragged herself into her cave and then flung herself on her bed. Between her pregnancy and the wretched emotions of the moment she could not sleep. She was unsure how long she lied there staring up at the ceiling.

* * * * *

Medusa's aimless thoughts of misery were interrupted by Georgios' loud squawking. Letting out a heavy sigh she did not move. There was absolutely no desire to move hitting her squarely. What reason did she even have to get up, least yet do anything? Georgios squawked even louder to let Medusa know that he was hungry. She had enough. Athena kept taking everything away from her. What would be the point of trying to carry on? That cruel goddess would just take it away again. She pulled herself off of her bed and dragged herself outside. Reaching out she knocked the bucket she had sitting on a rock over. It splashed grain all over the place with a very good amount of it going into her chicken pen. Medusa bent down to grab the sword that she had got from Athens before reaching out and opening her chicken pen.

Sadly she mumbled, "Goodbye my little friends."

Slowly and evenly she trudged away while making sure not to look back at what had become of Proetus. It was just too painful to see. After stomping along solemnly she came to the pond. Her mind immediately flashed back to her shaking hand the first time she bathed with him. Once again she started to cry. It was all so tiring. Medusa stepped into the pond with her sword in hand and her chiton still on. She stopped once the water was up just below her chest. The snakes on her head seemed to be unusually agitated as she got into the water. Glancing at the sword in her hand she realized what she was doing. She was going to end it all. It was unfair and cruel but she just could not do it anymore. Raising the sword up, she pointed it at herself. Tears welled once again as she paused. As she started to bring the sword down towards her chest one of the snakes on her head lashed out and bit her on the arm!

Medusa flailed her free hand at it and yelled out, "Owww!"

The snake released its hold on her arm as she swiped at it. Medusa refused to let the damned snakes stop her from ending this horrible excuse of a life that she had been forced to live. Raising the sword up again she tried to move quicker in stabbing herself. This time one of the snakes on her head wrapped itself around her hand where she was holding the sword. She strained to fight against it. Another snake wrapped itself around her forearm and a third one lashed out and sunk its fangs into her forearm. It hurt a lot more than she had thought it would. Struggling to fight against them she pushed the sword closer to her chest. Suddenly she felt something bump her from within her stomach. It confused her because she had never felt anything like it. Pausing to figure out what had happened caused her to stop straining against the snakes with her sword. Her hand was pulled away from her chest by the snakes. She accidentally dropped the sword. It happened again and she immediately realized exactly what it was. It was her baby moving in her stomach! The snakes holding her arm, including the one biting her forearm, released their grip on her. She moved her hand down to her stomach to pause and wait so she could feel her baby move yet again. After a bit of a wait the baby moved again and she felt it kicking against her left hand. Medusa started crying. She wanted to end it all but she could not bring herself to murder her baby.

CHAPTER 24

Bending over, Medusa picked up the sword that she had dropped into the pond. Slowly she trudged out of the pool soaking wet. Her arm hurt significantly where those damned snakes had bit her. She immediately realized that they were going to fight to keep her in this miserable existence. She was stuck since deep down inside she that could not end her own child. Especially since it was the only thing of Proetus that she had left. She fell to her knees and screamed out in frustration. Both anger and pain flowed through her as she hurled the sword into the forest. When would it be enough? She was desperate to know when she was allowed to be happy. Athena kept taking and taking. Suddenly it all hit her. It was all a joke. It had to be, no other way everything could have kept happening the way it was. Medusa started to laugh. She laughed heartily about it all. While laughing she pulled herself off the ground. Finally she recovered enough to look around. She spotted her sword that she had tossed lying on the ground. Strolling over to the sword she bent down and picked it up. Her growing belly was making it difficult to bend over but she was able to get the sword.

"Oh, I accidentally knocked over my bucket. I better go and clean that mess!" She said to no one in particular.

Walking as briskly as she could she headed back to her home to see her chicken were attacking the loose grain. Medusa set her sword down and then collected up the excess grain. Once she had as much as she could get she put the bucket back on its rock and closed the chicken pen.

While whistling away she set her hand on Proetus' cheek before saying, "Dear, our baby kicked today. It is quite exciting."

Glancing down at her chiton she noticed that it was covered at mud from her knees down.

"Oh my. It appears I have soiled my chiton. I want to look my best so if you will excuse me I will go wash it clean." Medusa told Proetus.

She paused to wait for his response before turning to head back towards the pond. After washing her chiton she returned to the cave. Her stomach rumbled with hunger so she changed her chiton and then made breakfast. She had not noticed it before but recently she had found herself ravished by hunger. It took almost as much food as she had been feeding Proetus to fill her own belly. It must have been the baby demanding to eat as well. Once she finished eating she was quite groggy, especially since she had not eaten since last night before going to Sami. Lying down on her bed she closed her eyes and sleep virtually assaulted her.

* * * * *

Pulling her bow back Medusa left fly an arrow and then watched as it struck true hitting a hare right in the chest. It turned to run and after a few steps flopped over on its side. She had become very skilled at using her bow. She had also become quite pregnant. It was about seven months along and she was just noticing that her agility was starting to become significantly affected. She waddled over to the hare and lifted it by its rear legs. Unfortunately she did not find any more during the day but at least this one would be enough for a few days. It was just past lunch so she decided to quit, especially since she was hungry. Ever since she became pregnant she found eating fish completely unacceptable. For some reason it only made her sicker. Because of that she generally ate only hare for meat. It was starting to concern her, maybe the hare were catching on to what she was doing because she was seeing less and less of them. Perhaps tomorrow she would try a new area to hunt them.

Suddenly as she took a few steps back towards the forest she heard a male voice call out, “Hey!”

Medusa startled before shifting to look in the direction of the voice. Moving along the edge of the forest and heading towards her she spotted a trio of men. Each was wearing a long-sleeved chiton that had a bronze metal plate shaped like a bare-chested man. They were all armed with spears and carrying a circular shield painted green with a sun emblem on it. Each had bronze helmets with a wide black feathered crest and openings in front of each eye that cut downwards to the mouth. From the knees down on each of their legs were shaped metal plates that covered their lower legs and feet to provide protection. It was very obvious to her that they were professional soldiers of some kind.

In reaction to her looking at them the man leading the three of them said, “Woman what are you doing out here alone?”

Medusa paused for a bit to think on it. She had forgotten that many women in cities were not allowed to be alone in public. She was just thankful that she had her himation on. It would have been very bad for her if they spotted her and she did not see them. Proetus would have been quite mad at her to have her killed, especially since she had their growing baby within her.

Deciding to try and talk her way out of the situation she answered, “I am a just out hunting for my family.”

As they approached one of the other men commented, “She is pregnant.”

“Where is your husband to hunt for you?” The man who seemed like their leader asked.

Not wanting them to know the truth she answered, “He is dead so I have to do it.”

The third man who had said nothing beforehand asked, “Have you seen any monsters?”

“What do you mean monsters?” She tried to ask in as a casual of a voice that she could pull off.

It was her that they were looking for. No doubt what she did to Athena’s temple in Sami had caught more than one person’s attention. The realization that she was going to have to move far away from this part of the island hit her. No doubt more of these soldiers would come hunting for her. Right now she did not think that she could move all of her things very fast, especially in her current condition. She decided to start scouting out for a spot tomorrow. Most likely the best place to look was far to the south. There was a lot less people living on that part of Kefalonia.

The men looked to each other before the one who she guessed was their leader answered, “Do you not know what happened in Sami?”

Realizing that it was best to feign ignorance so she replied, “I never go to Sami.”

“A hideous beast assaulted Athena’s temple and burned it to the ground. Somehow it turned all of the priestesses into statues and then escaped unseen.”

“That is horrible.” Medusa stated flatly.

“Yes it is. We must be off to continue our search.” The man told her.

“Okay.” She responded and then started to walk away.

As she took a single step away one of the men grabbed her arm before saying, “Wait.”

The leader of them announced, “We must see your face in order to insure you are innocent. Remove your himation.”

Medusa frowned. She had promised Proetus just last week that she would not turn anyone into stone. Breaking her promise so quickly was not something she wanted to do.

Deciding to try and talk them out of making her remove her himation she said, “It is not appropriate for you to be demanding such things of me. How do you think Athena would feel about you assaulting women by taking away their protections?”

The man who ordered her to remove her himation answered, “She would understand due to our motives.”

“Fine. I tried.” Medusa replied.

Pulling her arm out of the man’s hand she ripped off her himation to expose her face. The men all reacted with initial panic before recovering and clenching their spears upward. Before they could continue to move in what she assumed would be an assault they all started to turn to stone. Medusa shrugged because she tried her best to convince them to leave her alone. Wrapping her himation around her head once again, she headed off. The thought to push them over to try and hide the men crossed her mind but she just did not have the physical strength to do it. It took a bit longer to get back to her cave but once she got back she gutted and skinned her hare before sitting down next to Proetus.

"I have to apologize. I tried not to turn people to stone but these soldiers attacked me and I had no choice."

"It was not a wise choice. It could bring more men here."

"I know. After our baby is born I was thinking to move to the south. Tomorrow I will go and search out a spot. Maybe after that I will start to prepare the spot I find. You know, make a new garden and possibly start to set up a new pen for the chicken. What do you think?"

"A good plan."

She turned to look at him. He was still a stone statue turned towards her with a smile on her face. Reaching out she tenderly touched his cheek and smiled. While looking at him she noticed that he was getting a bit dirty from sitting there.

"I am going to make lunch. Also it looks like you need a bath. I will get your old chiton and use it to wash you if you do not mind."

Standing up she finished with the hare by cutting it into small strips to eat. She then made it into a stew with several vegetables and then served herself. The further along this pregnancy got the hungrier and hungrier she had got. Also her breasts seemed to be swelling inside and were beginning to leak milk. It would be a relief to get this baby out. Not only because she desperately wished to hold her baby but also because her lower back was starting to hurt. After she ate and cleaned up her mess she sat back down in her chair.

"Proetus I was thinking about names for our baby. If we have a boy I was thinking we could name him Philon and if we have a girl I was thinking of Thalia. What do you think?"

"They both sound wonderful."

Turning to grin at him she replied, "Thank you."

Medusa struggled for a moment but was finally able to pry herself out of her chair and stand.

"I will be right back." She told him before pulling his old chiton off of the chair.

It was a bit of a walk to the pond and her feet hurt quite a bit from all the walking. She flipped off her sandals and rose her chiton up around her waist to tie it in place. There was a large rock wedged into the side of the pond that she decided to sit on while dipping her feet into the cool water. It felt quite wonderful. It was going to be quite a journey to travel far enough south to find a new place to live. Reaching out she gave her left foot a rub. Off in the distance she heard something stumbling through the woods. She could hear the mumbling of voices in the distance so she knew that it was men. Moving quickly she stood up and walked back into the forest and then stopped to turn around so she was hidden behind the trees. Waiting with baited breath she watched carefully in the direction that she heard them coming from. After a bit of a nerve filled wait, a group of men appeared. They were walking in a long line with one man leading from the middle gestured for them to stop.

He turned towards the others and ordered, "Get some water. It is getting late and we will head back to Sami."

"What of the monster?"

The leader chuckled before declaring, "We have been searching since morning and tomorrow we will continue the search for it. If it is in this forest we shall find it."

"And what if it is not in this forest?"

"Then we will head to the next one."

She could tell that several of the soldiers seemed quite unhappy. The fact they planned to search the whole forest concerned her. She did not need them stumbling onto her cave and Proetus. Part of her thought to stand out from behind the trees and turn all of them to stone right here but remembering that they would be hovering over her private pond was more than a little uncomfortable to her. She did not need a bunch of men hovering over her while she bathed. In the end she decided to stay hidden and hope they would not find her cave. Plus, she did promise

Proetus not to be turning people into stone statues. How would it look if she purposely turned these men into statues so soon after doing it to the others? While staying behind her tree she watched as the men took turns getting some water before they reformed into a line and headed away. Based on their direction she guessed that they were headed towards Sami. It was quite a relief to her as she watched them leave. Once they were fully out of sight and she could no longer hear them moving she headed to her cave. Proetus was still waiting for her when she got back. Taking the wet chiton she slowly began to rub it along the dirt that was covering Proetus. She made sure to move his clean chiton in order to not get it wet.

"What took you so long?"

"A bunch of soldiers appeared at the pond searching for me. I hid behind a tree and waited until they left."

Slowly and evenly she cleaned Proetus before tossing the now both wet and dirty chiton onto the top of one of the posts of her chicken pen. Even after resting her feet in the pond she found they still hurt so she sat down in the chair to enjoy the day. She was unable to see the sun as it had set below the tree line and it was just starting to get dark. Pretty soon she was going to have to eat and go to sleep. Tomorrow she would begin her search for a new home. It just dawned on her that she was going to have to find some way to move Proetus to the new place once she found it. A task she did not look forward to. Maybe once she had the baby she would regain much of her strength and she could do it. For now it was time to eat and go to sleep.

CHAPTER 25

Medusa struggled to get out of bed as Georgios squawked loudly at her. She was so heavily pregnant that basic movement was becoming difficult. Over the last 2 months she had tried to store and dry as much food as possible to prepare for this time but she realized that she was not ready for the difficulty that being pregnant was causing her. She could hardly wait to get this damned baby out of her. Once she was on her feet she waddled out of her cave and fed her chicken. Her stomach rumbled in hunger. She glanced over at Proetus and saw his plate from dinner was still sitting on his lap.

"I guess you were not hungry? Let me clean that up for you and make breakfast." She told him.

He did not reply to her so she took it as a yes. Picking up his plate she dumped the waste into her small composting pile. At this point she finally found a perfect new spot. It was once again a cave but it was located along a small mountainside near the southern end of the island. The only part she did not like was the distance to clean water. There was not a nice pond like she had now but only a small stream running down the mountainside by the cave. She thought that maybe once these men stopped searching for her she could come back to this cave. It really was perfect for her. She had already moved most of her extra clothing and various items. Also she had built up her garden and the new chicken pen. Today she was planning to move as many of her plants as she could carry. It took her a third of her day to walk to her new location so she only could get one trip a day. After making breakfast she selected several plants to tuck away into her bag. She also would carry several plants. She flung her himation over her shoulder and turned to look at Proetus. He was still sitting in his chair looking at her chair. Setting down one of the plants she walked over to him and reached out with her hand to touch his cheek.

"I will be back once I plant these in the new garden. Tomorrow we are going to move the rest of the chicken to their new home. Then next our bed. I am afraid you cannot come until after our baby is born but once they are here I will try to find a way to bring you home too. I love you."

She turned and started to walk. It was a long distance so she made sure to stop at the pond to get a drink of water. Her feet, back, and sides all hurt from both being very pregnant and the walk. Before her pregnancy she could have made this walk in under a third of the time. There had to be plenty of breaks along the way for her to take a rest but she finally made it to the new cave. This cave was much bigger than her old one and it had a small tunnel that seemed to lead down further. The first day she found it she decided to block the tunnel off for safety so every time she visited she placed a few rocks over it. At this point she had blocked it off entirely and piled enough rocks over the pile that no one could ever get through it. The first thing she did as she walked up was to set down the plants and to feed her chicken that she had here. Anthousa was back at her old cave with Georgios and tomorrow she was going to move them. Tenderly as possible she removed each plant from her bag and then put them into the ground. Her garden was almost fully transferred. At this rate she was expecting her baby to be born in this new cave. All of the lessons that her mother gave her about childbirth had rattled through her head constantly over the last few months. Medusa had no idea how she was going to do it all by herself but she had no other choice. It was not as though a nursemaid was going to be willing to help someone like her give birth to who knew what. Shc sighed heavily. It was something that she was going to have to deal with very soon. Only two days ago she already had a false labor. It was immensely painful so she imagined that the actual thing was going to be horrible. Once she finished putting all of her new plants in the garden she slowly struggled to get back on her feet. Normal walking was something she was going to be quite happy for once she had this baby. After getting up she went to the nearby stream to wash both her hands and the bag that she brought with her. Her stomach rumbled with hunger so she went back to the cave and collected a few things to eat. It was just going to be some fruit and vegetables since all of her meat was back in the old cave. She shrugged it off and began to eat as she walked. Because of her hunger she gobbled down everything rather quickly. While it was not ideal, it satiated her enough. Just like the walk there she had to stop multiple times in order to rest. This time the breaks were much more frequent and lasted longer. Being pregnant was sapping the energy out of her. During the trip back she recognized the area close to her cave but her feet hurt so much she had to stop and rest.

While rubbing her feet Medusa complained to no one in particular, "Proetus I will get you back for making me go through this."

She could hear another loud group of what she guessed were men searching the forest. It was slowly getting worse and worse. She had been able to avoid them very effectively. Sitting quietly she realized that they were behind her and heading towards her. Crawling to her feet she began to walk towards the cave. Her hope was to be able to get out of sight quickly, especially since sunset was rapidly approaching. While walking she realized that she could hear the men approaching from both behind her and off to her right. They were expanding their search and she was about to be trapped. Off in front of her she spotted her cave so she tried to pick up the pace enough to get there. Moving rapidly she slipped her himation off her shoulder and wrapped it around her head quickly.

Right as she entered the cave she heard a male voice call out, "Someone just went into that cave!"

She sighed heavily. The last thing that she wanted to deal with was a bunch of men harassing her. It was dark enough in the cave that she knew they could not see her so she turned around and watched. The men who came into view and formed up in front of her cave appeared to be wearing the same armor as the ones she turned to stone a few months ago. No doubt they were part of the same group. Maybe they even discovered those men and it might explain why so many more were there. Taking a quick count she counted nine of them. They slowly spread out and were ready to fight.

A man's loud voice called out, "We saw you go in there. Come out now or we will come in."

Letting out a deep sigh she realized that there would be no way for her to avoid this. It however completely changed her timetable. She was going to have to spend all day tomorrow moving everything she had left here to her new home.

Calling out in a fake scared voice she said, "I am just a homeless girl please do not molest me."

The same man who yelled earlier replied, "You are no girl. We can see a victim of your evil magic right there in front of us!"

Dang it! She thought to herself. Proetus was still just sitting in that chair and they saw him. At this point she realized that there was nothing she could do. The men knew what she was and they intended to hurt her. Slowly she unwrapped her himation and dropped it to the floor of the cave. It was time to deal with these men once and for all. After all, she just wanted to be left alone.

As she stepped out of the cave one of the men called out, "By the gods, it is hideous."

The leader of them ordered, "Steady men, approach it with caution."

Medusa grinned wickedly before slowly turning her gaze from man to man. They stood no chance as their own caution caused each one of them to slowly approach her before being turned to stone. When she finally glanced at the last man he started to turn to run but he made the mistake of looking into her eyes as he moved. He froze to stone and then fell over due to the unbalance of his position.

Medusa shook her head disappointedly before turning to Proetus and saying, "I am sorry dear. I just want us to be left alone but no one seems to want to leave us. Tomorrow I will move to our new home and once the baby is born I will come back for you."

Giving him a little pat on his cheek Medusa set her bag down on her chair. Through all of this her hunger had grown immensely. She was ready to eat dinner, especially after such a light lunch. She cooked herself some eggs and hare before getting a few figs. She had planted a young fig tree next to the new cave so she had to borrow these figs from an orchard nearby. It was a pleasant surprise to find the orchard by the new cave and very much helped make her feel better about moving there. As she ate the figs it reminded her of her time in Athens and the young lady who helped her. Medusa had not thought of her in so long that she forgot her name at first. Suddenly she remembered the name of the girl. It was Agnodice. She wondered what had happened to that girl back in Athens. It was one of the many things that Medusa knew that she would never know about. Shrugging off her old memories Medusa set her plate down and then went to go get the book that she had bought for her child. Every few nights she would read a few pages to Proetus. Mostly she did it because she knew that Proetus liked it but also she wanted to make sure that she could read well enough to teach their child. Cracking open the book as she sat down, she picked right back up where she had left off. At this part of the book it was talking about how Zeus was always cheating on his wife with beautiful mortal women. It seemed to be something that all of the male gods did regularly. They would manipulate, rape, or kill mortal women who did not do their bidding and throw themselves at the gods. Medusa was as much a victim of that as the women in these stories. She felt quite disgusted thinking about the look on the face of the old man who turned out to Poseidon. He was a disgusting creature and she imagined the other gods were no better. Sighing heavily she stood up. Tomorrow was going to be a long day. She would have to make at least three more trips in order to get the rest of her things safely to the new cave. The first item she decided to take was going to be her bed. It was just cloth and wool so she could simply drag it there with one arm while holding her bag filled with a few things. After a long nice stretch she bent over and gave Proetus a soft kiss on the cheek.

"Good night my love. I will see you tomorrow."

She headed into the cave and after settling down she drifted off to sleep.

* * * * *

Medusa was startled awake by the sound of her chicken squawking angrily about something. She sat up and looked out towards the entrance of her cave. An obviously male figure was blocking most of the outside light from entering the cave. He was wearing an unusual cap, what looked like leather armor, winged shoes, holding a sword in one hand and a very large unusual looking shield in the other. For some reason she could not see any more than the shadowy figure of the man.

Standing up she nervously asked, "Who are you?"

The man shifted his shield towards her and then looked into the shield.

He boldly stated, "I am Perseus and I am here to end you monster."

Medusa panicked. The man was not looking at her so there was no way that she could turn him to stone. She sidestepped to get away from him.

"Go away, I did nothing to you." She yelled out at him.

"You need not 'do' anything beast. I need your head as a gift."

Looking to her left and right she struggled to find something to defend herself. The nearest thing that she could find was an old battered sword sitting against the wall next to the shadowy man. He began to move closer towards her and raised his sword.

Pleadingly she attempted to explain, "I am no monster."

The man laughed before declaring, "Of course you are. Look at you. So hideous. Your head will make a prize that will thrust me into the annals of history."

"I am a woman cursed not a monster."

"I do not care what you think you are. My needs are greater than your life."

Trying to convince him she stated, "I am pregnant with my child."

"Only more reason to end you." He declared.

He took a few more steps closer. Medusa shifted away and towards the wall behind her. Grabbing a nearby jar filled with water she tossed it at the man. It shattered against his shield, which she realized was mirrored. She now knew how he was able to see her without turning to stone. Trying to back away from him she bumped into the back wall of the cave.

"Please just leave me alone, I just want to be left alone." She wailed out in desperation.

"You end now." The man angrily declared.

She spotted a flash of light flicker off to her right and then everything went black.

EPILOGUE

Proetus lurched slightly forward as his eyes cleared once again. It took him a moment to brush off the unusual gray fog that seemed to lift from around him. He found it odd that he was sitting in a chair facing an empty chair. After his initial stun he shifted to look around. He suddenly remembered where he was. He was on a small farm outside of a cave in the middle of a forest. Medusa! His mind rushed back to her. The last thing that he remembered was seeing a flash of light and then turning to see her. It was all true. Medusa was indeed cursed as a monster with snake hair. Where did she go to? The last that he had saw was her. She was sitting in the chair that he was looking at. He heard several confused voices come from nearby. Glancing out into the forest he spotted movement in the dark. It was several men wearing bronze armor. Specifically they looked like Corinthians. Concern suddenly hit him as he wondered where Medusa had gone to. Struggling to his feet, which seemed sluggish, he stood up.

"Medusa?" He called out hoping to catch her attention.

As he took his first step into the cave a man came barreling out. He was wearing an unusual leather helmet, treated leather armor, winged shoes and a very large mirrored bronze shield. In his right hand he was carrying a bag that appeared wet. Proetus watched him as he briskly kept walking and before long disappearing out of sight. A wave of panic began to form as Proetus' groggy malaise fully lifted. Turning towards the cave he jogged in.

"Medusa!" He called out trying to get her attention.

His fears were immediately realized true when he spotted her lying on the ground up against one of the walls. He could see a pool of blood all around her. Running as fast as he could he knelt down next to her and placed his hands on her arm. It was then that he realized that her head was missing. That bastard cut her head clean off! Leaning forward Proetus pressed his forehead on her arm and rested his hands on her chest and now very pregnant belly. He began sobbing. Whoever did this to her would pay! As he was prone over her dead body he felt something move under his hand that was resting on her belly. Lifting his head up he looked at his hand and immediately realized what it was. It had to have been his child! Fear hit him. His child was probably slowly dying in her womb. Looking around he spotted the sword that Medusa had let him use many times. Proetus moved as quickly as he could by first igniting a torch and then grabbing the sword. What he was about to do was very barbaric but he had no choice. Using the sword he slowly cut off her chiton and then cut through her skin. After a few very tense and delicate moments he was able to cut open her womb. The baby's voice echoed out in a loud bawling cry. Proetus had saved his child. The first thing he noticed was the baby appeared normal. Oddly enough the child seemed to have blue eyes. He remembered her telling him that she had blue eyes. He tossed the sword aside and ran to collect both a clean chiton and some water. As he plucked the child from out of her womb he realized that it was a boy. It was still bawling loudly. Using some water he rinsed the baby off and then wrapped it with the chiton to protect it. With his sight restored Proetus decided that he would go home to Argos.

As he stepped out of the cave he turned to his newborn son and said, "Son I shall name you after the sorrow I feel… Megapenthes."

He paused to look around. There was no one there. Deciding it was best to at least bury Medusa's remains, he set Megapenthes down on one of the chairs and got the sword that he used to cut out his son. It took him some time to dig a hole for her. Once he did, he buried her body and then stabbed the sword into the ground to act as a marker.

Scooping up the swaddled baby Proetus turned towards the open forest and declared, “Son, let us go home and claim my throne.”

THANK YOU!

I'd like to thank the many people who helped to make this book happen. First and foremost I'd like to thank God. Without the inspiration of our maker I could never write so frequently. As always my wife Parneeta keeps me going as I continue to create new worlds in these stories. My three little ones, Shawn II, Spencer, and Astir who are the center of my universe. I would like to thank Howard Pak for creating the amazing cover. To my friends Kathryn, Antti, and Melissa for your excitement in this story. It greatly helped push me to continue writing it. Lastly, but most importantly, you the reader. Thank you.

ABOUT THE AUTHOR

Born in Muskegon, MI and raised in Concord, CA, S.W. Gunn used his early experience as a roleplaying geek to expand upon his imagination. Unable to purchase the proper Dungeon and Dragons manuals at a young age, he developed his own roleplaying paper and pen game for himself and his friends to play. While living in Hawaii, he completed his Bachelor's in Art degree in History at Chaminade University of Honolulu. He is married to his lovely wife Parneeta and they have three wonderful children, Shawn (2nd), Spencer, and Astir. They live in Tacoma, WA.

OTHER WORKS BY THIS AUTHOR:

The Heima Series:
- Heima: The Ninth Kostir
- Heima: Challenge to the Crown
- Heima: Neinn

The Legenda Series:
- Smuggler's Luck
- Gift of Flight

Acciaccato
The Almighty Paw
The Priestess Princess
Angels of Evernal
Skybound

Made in the USA
Monee, IL
21 July 2023

39692384R00116